I0587103

Metal Angels

By

D K Girl

Metal Angels by D K Girl

Cover Design: Jake Clark
Editor: Inspired Ink Editing
ISBN-13: 978-0-9981427-7-7

For Mikie.

You should be here.

KIRA - 1

Kira raised her metal fist and sang her booze-soaked heart out to the ceiling. The music blaring in the pub downstairs made the whole room vibrate. She hit the high note. God damn nailed it.

'Christ almighty.' The guy beside her rolled his generous package away, and grunted out of bed. 'You could kill small animals with that voice, K.'

'I don't pay you to talk, Liam.' Kira tossed a pillow at his smirking, pudgy face, and the room spun. 'Be gone. I'm done with your dimpled ass.'

She was up for a lot of things, but her rent-a-fuck seeing her puke wasn't one of them, and any second now a bolt to the bathroom would be compulsory.

Liam pulled on his pants, gave her the finger, and launched that smile. Honey on warm toast. He may have a gut you could eat breakfast off, but damn, that grin. It made his grey eyes gleam, and wrenched ridiculously high tips from her blacker-than-black credit card.

'Till next time.' He stepped into the hall, the blast of music deafening before he pulled the door closed.

Kira sighed. Her nipples were on full alert under the touch of the breeze coming through the wide-open windows. She arched her back, sending her boobs skyward, but even that small movement made her gut twist.

'Fuck. Nope, no way. Stay down. Sangria and whisky you need to be better friends.' She reached for her underwear, slivers of sapphire-red material lying on the timber floor. Carefully, super carefully, she pulled the delicate g-string up over her thighs. Satin bra next. She'd learned a lesson early on about the metal prosthetic she called a right arm. It didn't think much of Victoria's Secrets. The 'armadillo'—what Kira called the intricate folds of hard metal that moved with the smoothness of oil on skin— existed on a diet of lace and satin, always managing to catch threads between its layers and refusing to let go. The bastard thing had cost her a fortune in the beginning, but three years on Kira had it under control. Even at times like now, when her vision was blurry, and the room tilted and lurched like a motherfucker.

She stood up, defying gravity. Jeans on, zip done. A

god-damn dressing genius. Shirt proved an issue. Whose fucking idea had it been to buy something with more holes than material? It took three tries to find the armholes; two of those attempts ending up with her flat on her back. Sangria and whisky held hands, waiting patiently at the base of her throat.

'Jesus. Perry's going to kill me.'

Nothing new there. It was pretty much his permanent state. And yet the crazy son of a bitch had agreed to partner with her in the Wheel and Barrow. She was supposed to be downstairs right now, behind the bar. She'd promised Perry she'd cover the midnight-till-three shift, but her promises were as empty as the fishtank in their musty back office. Thankfully, the guy was practically some kind of Sri Lankan saint. Never bitched at her when she ditched the whole damn town of Pryden on a whim and flew off to Greece, or somewhere equally stupidly beautiful, just because she was Kira Beckworth and she could. And his lips remained sealed on nights like this. When she drank too much of the stock and decided small talk with drunk-ass customers was overrated, and that a quick session was in order instead.

Liam didn't cost top dollar for nothing; but damn, it made the room stink. She sniffed her armpits. Sweet Jesus, the room wasn't the only thing. Kira focused on the door like a magnifying glass on an ant and found her way out into the hall, up the short flight of stairs to the fire exit, and out onto the rooftop. The night sky was velvet black, dotted with hundreds of diamonds, and the breeze coming in off the desert pushed goosebumps to attention across every centimetre of her skin.

Kira raised her arms to the view. 'Fuck yes.'

The town of Pryden was a small blob of light in the wide expanse of curving, undulating sand hills that spread out forever around it. Somewhere off to the east and hidden in the crux of a mountain range was the Facility. And in that sterile, high-tech, boring-as-bat-shit place sat Kira's sister, Blake.

The great and wondrous Blake Beckworth. The goddess of bioengineering. The reason anyone paid Kira two shits of attention. The gossip mags had fallen in love with the idea that nothing about Kira was real. That her grief-stricken genius sister Blake had created a masterpiece in her biotech nirvana after the car accident: an android version of her dead sis to dull the pain.

Yeah, right. The sisters both knew Kira wasn't the one Blake would have resurrected if the aliens had actually said yes to using a shitload of their precious, funky metal to play 'build a likeness.' Dear old Dad would have been walking the halls again instead. No question. But the world didn't know that. And apparently it was a thing now, trying to get into Kira's pants to see if she had a robo-muff. Kira flashed her lady garden on a regular basis to prove she didn't. She was a real girl, god-damn it. But her plan had backfired. The press loved a crazy rich bitch. Especially one whose rarely-sighted, brainiac sister was holed up in a place whose security and secrecy were whispered about on a regular basis. No one gave a shit about Area 51 anymore; it was all about the Facility.

'And sometimes conspiracy theory nutcases are right,' Kira told the night sky.

She tilted her prosthetic back and forth. The moon was a giant half-ball of silver light, but the armadillo didn't give a fuck. When light hit the metal it kind of soaked in, dulling down to something insipid and barely there at all. Like a five-fingered black hole. Her heart was made of the same stuff. The chunk of metal in her chest didn't beat, didn't flutter, didn't race. Brilliant as they all may be—Blake and her little extra-terrestrial friends—they were also assholes. They had tech that had guided them all the way from their universe to this pissy one, yet they couldn't come up with a way to make her heart beat? Even if it was pretend? And what was with the no fingernails on the armadillo? Smooth nubs. Just bloody creepy.

Sure, Blake had put fingernails into the faux skin she wanted Kira to wear over the prosthetic, but there was as much chance of Kira wearing that fucking awful sheath as there was of her getting to the gym this week. Or of Blake actually calling to see how the hell her sister was.

Kira fixed her eyes on the stars overhead. One in particular, a bright little splat directly above them. The rest of the universe rotated around it in a slow, torturous circle. She braced against the back of a faded chaise lounge, determined to keep looking. Something about the wide-open space, the endlessness overhead, never failed to give her the feels. If she could, she'd jump into that nothingness and let it take her. Let it swamp her, suck her down into the black hole that was already a part of her. The one she should have stayed in after the car crash.

Sangria and whisky hit the back of her throat in treacherous unison, and there was no stopping the evacuation this time. Deep red vomit made preschooler paintings on the concrete. Wiping her mouth, Kira sighed.

'Such a waste.' She straightened, throat tingling with the sting of bile. 'Okay, let's do this. Perry is going to shit kittens if I don't help out. K, you've totes got this.'

And after three attempts at the door-handle, she did. Stairs were trickier. *Who the fuck put oil on these bastards?* The music from the pub made the wooden stairwell vibrate, meaning no one heard her screech when the third step from the bottom rose up and slapped her on the ass. Kira punched it, metal on wood. No contest. The step suffered the loss of a chunk, splinters spiking out like broken bone. With the pain receptors on the prosthetic set to their lowest level, Kira grinned and gave the nasty woodwork a one-fingered salute. The music shut off at the same moment.

'Kira, are you okay? Where are your shoes?'

Kira jerked, her spine slamming against the next step up. 'Fuck, Perry, you trying to make me piss my pants?'

The man standing over her rolled his eyes. 'You handle that quite well on your own. Thanks for covering the shift for me, silly cow.'

Damn that accent was god damn heavenly, rising up and going down like one of those pretty wooden ponies on a carousel.

'I was just coming to take over,' she said.

'The bar just closed.'

'Why did you close it so early?'

'Oh bloody hell, Kira.' Perry sighed, but there was a flash of pearly whites. Kira pursed her lips, moved in for a kiss, but Perry screwed up his face. 'Shit, you stink. Kira, listen to me.'

'No. I own more shares in this place than you do, so shut your pretty mouth.'

'Bitch.' More pearly whites, bright as a damn supernova. The dude needed to ease up on the whitening treatments.

'Don't you forget it,' Kira said. 'Talk to me, P-man. Tell me about rainbows and kittens.'

Sweetness and light were good. They chased back the darkness. Darkness sucked balls. Way down here, at the bottom of the bottle, it had a harder time reaching her, but she wasn't always as invisible as she'd like. Perry gripped her hands, his slender fingers making hers look like chunky sausages.

'K, I've got to tell you something and I don't think you're going to love it,' Perry said.

Kira touched her flesh fingers to his sculpted beard. Jet-black bristles against fawn skin. Match made in heaven. 'You're pretty. I'm going to buy you a boyfriend.'

'I know, you keep saying, but I can find my own. Thanks anyway.' Perry swiped away another attempt to touch him. 'K, focus. Rossiter called.'

This was one of those times when a heart would thump. 'Why the fuck would He-Man do that?'

Built like a brick shithouse, Rossiter was Blake's not-so-friendly bodyguard. Admittedly, the man was an impressive chunk of Samoan Canadian manhood, with an impossibly shiny and smooth bald head.

'Blake wants you at the Facility,' Perry said.

Wasted to sober in warp speed. She slumped against Perry, and her cheek found the solid warmth of his chest. Being a short-ass had its advantages sometimes. A resting place where she could gather thoughts that had just scattered like dropped marbles. Never huge on conversations, Blake had offered her nothing but a rare hello for near on twelve months, dropping even that for absolute silence since the whole Eron thing.

The Eron thing.

Seriously, what the hell was the big deal with taking an alien off-site? The dude was bored shitless in that place. If they all wondered why it hadn't taken much for Kira to persuade Eron to go against his precious captain's orders and sneak out, management needed to take a good look at the entertainment line-up for the Facility. Once upon a time the aliens had been hired out as some kind of crack SWAT team. The occasional 'mission impossible'. Sold to the purchaser as fucking super-soldiers. It gave the ETs something to do, and people paid top dollar for 'genetically-enhanced humans' to clean up their shit. But that hadn't happened in a year or so. And polishing your own armour got real boring. Real fast. And, oh man, Eron had such nice pieces of armour.

Shit. Kira ground her forehead into Perry's chest. *Don't go there. No. Nope.*

'Kira, did you hear me?' Perry cradled her tight against his body, lifting her off the ground and moving them both down the hall. The guy was slender as a reed, but strong as a fucking ox. Kira was also practically an Oompa-Loompa which made things easier.

'Your words don't compute,' she told his chest hair. This part sucked harder than a Dyson. Not being able to tell Perry about the shit that went on behind the very, very high gates of the Facility. Even her best buddy thought the place did just what it said on the label, 'engineering and robotics design'. Perry had no idea that willowy guy with the impossible-to-look-away-from lips she'd brought in a couple of times was even more out of this world then he appeared.

'This is a good thing right? Blake wants to see you.' Perry grunted his way through a couple of doorways and the smell of stale liquor hit Kira square in the nostrils, making an unstable belly even more so.

'Probably just to ream me for maxing out the credit cards.' Kira shrugged.

But Blake wasn't calling her in at four in the morning to chat about credit cards. Kira had been fastidiously spending her share of Facility profits since the moment she'd woken up with a prosthetic arm, unbeating artificial heart, and irreparably guilty conscience; and her sister never said a word. Anything to keep Kira out of her hair, out of her life, Blake grabbed at.

'Jesus, K.' A lock of Perry's product-laden hair slipped over his forehead. 'Help me a little here. Walk.'

Somehow she did. One bare foot in front of the other. Where the hell were her shoes?

Perry did not lie. In the alleyway beside the pub sat a sleek white vehicle, one gull-wing door raised for her arrival. Giving her no time to escape, Perry shoved one of his favoured jackets at her - a glorious vinyl I'm-trying-to-be-badass creation with studs and all. He tapped the gull-wing and waved at her as it slid down and locked her in a sweet-smelling, beige leather prison.

'Asshole!' she shouted at the closed window. Something burned deep in her belly. This hangover was going to suck on a monstrous scale.

The automated vehicle rolled forward, taking a left out of the alleyway and heading out of town. Pryden was barely fit to be called a town, just a single main street with a sprinkling of suburbs around it, and by the time Kira had hauled herself upright again they'd hit the outer limits and cruised into the desert. A liquorice strip of road ran ahead, disappearing into the burnt-orange bumps of the desert. The road took a couple of twists and turns, then ran dead straight for twenty kilometres, all the way to the first security gate of the Facility. The faintest hint of powder-pink blush stained the horizon. Time for vampires to be heading indoors. Kira opened the window, ignoring the posh English-accented voice that advised her not to, so as to retain optimised conditions within the vehicle.

'Fuck you, car lady.' Kira hung her head out the window and the knots in her already mussed-up hair had triplets. The chill in the air from earlier had disappeared under the more familiar heavy warmth of the approaching day. Car lady was right, it wasn't optimal out here but Kira would be damned if she'd admit defeat to an autonomous vehicle. She narrowed her eyes against the blast of rushing air. Rossiter had the car set to a nice little pace. Whatever Blake wanted, she wanted it in a hurry. For ten minutes Kira enjoyed the fresh air pummelling her nostrils.

A tinkling of bells announced the rise of a screen on the dashboard.

'Answer.' Her every wish was the car's command. And every wish could be uttered without going anywhere near the steering wheel. Kira and driving were not good friends. Even sober. When Kira drove, people died.

A familiar face filled the screen. Rossiter, the incredibly annoying hulk. Kira tucked her feet up on the seat and nodded to him over the top of her knees. The dude had an enviable talent of raising one dark eyebrow, a talent he was showing off to full effect right now.

'Kira.'

'Good morning, Rossiter, you beautiful slab of man.'

Spittle flew from her mouth, onto the screen. Right over Rossiter's left eye. She laughed and instantly regretted not taking a bathroom break before leaving the bar.

'You're still drunk.' Rossiter regarded her with stony hazel eyes, and the eyebrow danced.

'It's four on a Saturday morning, what the hell else would I be?' Kira dragged her gaze from the gymnastic disapproval of the eyebrow and glanced outside. Up ahead loomed the low mountain range that ringed the Facility. 'What the fuck is going on? Why is Queen B summoning me? I'm busy as shit.'

'I don't question Blake's requests.' Rossiter lifted his planet-wide shoulders in a surprisingly delicate shrug. 'I just follow them.'

'Okay, whoa, I don't need to know about your special, private body-guarding stuff. Keep that in the bedroom.'

'Are you finished being juvenile?' His eyebrow was at full attention. Quite impressive.

'Probably?' Alcohol and unease gurgled in Kira's stomach. 'Am I?'

'Yes. You are. Now pay attention.' The big guy had a habit of going all boot-camp instructor on her. She blamed steroids. Usually. Today, though, he seemed less irritated and more distracted. He kept darting a look at a tablet he held.

'Attention being paid, sir.' She saluted him.

Hulk-Rossiter had a button nose that was almost adorable, especially now when he screwed it up. 'You need to get down there while the spacemen are at prayers.'

Curiosity surfed over trepidation, and Kira leaned forward. The aliens held a prayer service every morning at five, like clockwork. Their captain, a.k.a Mr Asshat, made them pray to some god of theirs for an hour. Eron had never given details, and Kira didn't want them. Other things to do.

To him. To his bits. And then him to her bits.

Shit, damn it, shit. Don't go there.

'You do know that's kind of…racist…or alienist…or something,' she said. 'It pisses them off, calling them spacemen.'

Eron had told her he hated the word. Almost as much as he hated being poked in the belly in the mornings. But it was so irresistible. His belly, not the word. Just the right mix of muscle and softness. So silky. And as for what lay lower, well hello sailor. Whatever moisturiser they used on that planet of theirs, Syrana, she needed the formula.

Holy Christ in chains, what was wrong with her? Sober up.

'Kira, pay attention for god's sake. The car will take you to the Quartermain entrance, I'll meet you there. Once the spacemen are at service, I'll take you to Blake on level eleven. '

'Roger that.' Kira saluted him again. 'Whoa, hang on a gosh-darned second. Level eleven?'

Two kilometres underground,with far more concrete and rock and steel between fresh air and freedom than she cared for. Made her chest tight thinking about it.

'See you at Quartermain in fifteen.' Rossiter signed off, leaving her glaring at a black screen.

'Dick!' Kira slumped into her seat, and the bongo drums in her head grew louder. Level eleven. Jesus. Kira hated being under bedcovers, let alone underground.

The car shot past her all-time favourite tree. A lone cactus, giving a one-fingered salute to the world in a giant, prickly display of defiance; set far apart from its clustered brothers and sisters that formed packs across the desert landscape.

Sighting the rebel of the cacti world meant the first of the Facility's security gates was about a minute away. The hired guns behind blackened windows would watch her speed past, aware she was coming from the moment Perry had shoved her into the car. A drone had probably filmed her throwing up on the roof-top. Hell, one had probably filmed Liam's liaison with her vagina. Keeping big secrets at the Facility meant stealing everyone else's.

Kira flopped across the back seat. 'Home sweet fucking home.'

ERON - 2

Eron opened his eyes to an emerald world, and awesome, terrible dread filled him.

'*Brandis mer.*' The Syranian curse flew from his lips with the sharpness of an arrow.

There were two places he should not be at this present point in time. Lahar's shrine on level nine, in the depths of the Facility's underground, was one of them. Yet, here Eron lay, intolerable fool that he was. Splayed out like a carcass at the base of the petrified tree stump that took pride of place at the centre of the Syranians' place of worship. Banished from the proceedings of the evening past, Eron's intention to spend a quiet few hours in repentant prayer had taken a toll. His eyes had closed, and, beyond all comprehension, he had slept.

Flickers of green light shimmered against the glass walls and ceiling and danced across his pale skin. Eron moved to rise, lifting his long limbs. Sudden and shocking pain halted him. It was as though ice had found its way into blood and bone and broken into untold numbers of razor-like shards. The level of discomfort was unfamiliar, a far distant memory from a life he barely recalled. Eron's appointment as one of the god Lahar's holy soldiers brought with it a preternatural tolerance for pain and a remarkable capacity for healing. But the only thing remarkable now was the level of agony he endured. Eron dragged himself the short distance to the nearest wall, pressing elongated fingers against the cold glass and using the leverage to raise himself to his feet. He got to his knees and could go no further. Though the Waters did not touch his skin directly – running as they did within the glasswork – the fluid's power reached inside him with taloned fingers and radiated beneath his pale flesh. The mighty and divine Waters were, as the humans would say, liquid gold. A flowing, transcendental medium that had once, a very long time ago, enabled the gods to move between their realm and the corporeal universes of Earth and Syrana. But for any mortal foolish enough to taste it, the liquid brought no hint of what it felt like to be divine – only a short-lived, desperately painful, and soul-crushing high.

Eron stared up at the domed roof of the shrine and forced a breath through the intolerable spasms. Carved into the glass above him was Lahar's glaring totem. A Precon beast from Eron's home planet, Syrana.

'Forgive me,' he breathed. His tongue betrayed him with human words, but he couldn't find the strength to admonish himself. The Precon eyed him with nothing resembling forgiveness. They were creatures feared for their inherent cruelty, known to leave prey hovering on the brink of death whilst they consumed it. The priests of Syrana's temples had chosen well for divine Lahar. As one of the last three Living Gods—deities still tethered to the corporeal worlds—Lahar's desperation to rise to the next realm bred a cruelty that had seen Eron's home planet embroiled in war for the entirety of his memory, and beyond. It was this same desperation that had brought Eron and his brothers to Earth. Lahar had aligned himself with the goddess Ereshkigal, a diety long since moved to the next realm, in the hope that his own transcendence would be his reward. Eron had been forced to leave his world behind for a god that wanted nothing more than to abandon them altogether.

The goddess's totem watched Eron too. An Arabian wolf whose enormous eyes let nothing go unnoticed. The air was thick and freezing in Eron's nostrils, his breathing challenged. God-soldier or not, he'd lingered far too long in close proximity to these Waters. The body-hugging shirt he wore insulated him against natural temperature fluctuations, but a very unnatural chill enveloped him now. Limbs weak, he knelt on hands and knees. Eron blinked against the lights in his vision, fighting the encroachment of unconsciousness. Cold splinters made light work of his innards, and his bones were brittle with the chill. It would be no surprise to feel the taste of his own blood in his mouth, for it seemed that he was being jabbed within by a thousand angry points. A train of self-deprecating thoughts pounded their way through his mind. Ludicrous that it had come to this. He'd survived divine anointment and travelled breathtaking distances across space, only to freeze to death in his own god's shrine while repenting.

A divine shower stall. That is what Kira had called the shrine when he'd made an ill-advised decision to bring her here. Eron groaned, pressing his hands against the glass. Of all the moments to allow the very reason for his alienation into his head, this surely was the most inopportune. He had spent the night here because he could not be elsewhere. Unable to stand alongside his god-soldier brothers at the First Meld. And Kira was the reason for his banishment from that sacred ceremony. She had put him here. Away from his brethren. Disenfranchised. Shut out of the very task that brought him to this world. But despite all his inner ragings her image refused to leave his mind. The human girl, with her wandering hands and soft mouth, had bewitched him.

Fingers gripped Eron's upper arms, and his shoulders were lifted from the ground.

'Eron, do you hear me?'

He recognised Bel's deep Syranian tone. Eron let his eyes flutter open. Bel stood over him, his outline silhouetted by a soft green glow, his ebony skin morphing him into a shadow.

'I hear you.' Eron's reply clicked with the rapidity of his native Syranian tongue.

Bel crouched down, lifting one of Eron's arms and draping it across his shoulder.

'Stand, Eron. Get to your feet.'

The world was darkening. Eron's thoughts with it. He didn't make a sound as he was lifted to his feet, Bel taking his weight across his shoulders. Their progress down the short flight of stairs, out of the shrine and into the greater expanse of the Orientation Room, was an ungraceful affair. Eron's weight was no issue, there being far too little of it, but his height and disabled body were. All the Syranians were tall in comparison to the humans, but Eron was the tallest of the group by a good half metre. Bel cursed under his breath as he tried to negotiate Eron's barely cooperating limbs. They reached the floor and Bel released him. Eron's knees met the concrete.

'How long have you been in there, you fool?' Bel said. 'Are you without any sense?'

A moot question that Eron did not answer. At least his breath came now without the sensation of knives slicing through his filtering cavity. He lifted his head. Bel was alone. No sign of the captain, or any other. That should have gladdened him, but he didn't have the energy or inclination for such an emotion. A dark, inky feeling embraced him. He'd come down here last night to slip out of the grip of isolation, to distract himself from his exclusion. It seemed the shrine had merely enhanced his depression.

'I do not need assistance.'

Eron's attempt to stand betrayed him, but to his utter relief, Bel did not offer further physical assistance.

'That is not what I have seen for some time, Eron,' Bel retied his loosened jet-black hair, as always pulling it tight enough to lift the skin around his eyes. 'You are lucky it was I who came to begin preparations for service this morning. Parator and Gren might not have been so amenable.'

The Orientation Room was a sparsely furnished space with bare walls and floors and Bel's voice seemed to reach every corner.

'A veridical observation.' Eron clutched at the back of one of only two chairs available. 'I thank you for your assistance, Bel.'

Eron's curiosity about the First Meld's success or

failure burned him to a degree not dissimilar to the Waters. Lifting a shaking hand, he pushed back a strand of silver hair escaped from a careless topknot. If the Meld was successful, a creature of Kur now stood in this world after thousands of years of absence. Bel's eyes rested on Eron, and there was a noticeable softness in the gaze. Of all his Syranian brethren, Bel seemed the least troubled by Eron's indiscretions with Kira. There was every chance he might answer Eron's enquiry.

'I understand how difficult last evening must have been for you,' Bel said. 'To be kept from the First Meld is no small thing. But this behaviour will see you no closer to inclusion, brother. You must get a hold of yourself. Show yourself to be worthy, if there is to be any hope you will be allowed presence at the Melding of the Four.'

Eron nodded. *Breathe.* Bel's voice gave him something to focus on. Breathe deeper. The chill seeped from him. The Waters released their hold. Believing himself steady enough, Eron released his tight grip on the chair. A rush of vertigo swept over him, and the room tilted. Bel grasped Eron by the elbow and applied just enough force to keep him upright. Turning to thank him, Eron noticed Bel's gaze drop to the small tattoo Eron bore on his right wrist: a small stain of black against translucent white skin. The tattoo he'd chosen on that final night out with Kira, three months ago. Eron liked dogs.

Small ones, of course. The very first evening he'd left the Facility with Kira, they'd happened across an old, thankfully near-sighted man walking his animal companion. The creature had not run from Eron; it had licked him, fallen asleep in his lap. It had wanted to be near him. Even now the memory still bestowed an odd calm. Despite what had ensued.

'These past weeks I have done nothing but serve my penance, Bel.' Eron pulled his arm away, hiding his wrist at the small of his back, keeping the proof of his inadequacy from sight. When he had been discovered by the captain, Eron had been as high as the proverbial Earthly kite after an evening spent in a place of music and flashing light. A place where his own oddness had been misconstrued and embraced by the humans around him, mingling with their own. A place where he could indulge his predilection for the finery and delicacy of the clothing of Earth's females without remonstration.

'You need to leave, Eron. You cannot be here when they arrive for service. They will be here within the half hour.'

Bel stooped to pick up the jacket Eron had discarded at the foot of the stairs hours ago. Eron chose to risk his question.

'Was the First Meld completed?' Eron said. 'Will you tell me that much, Bel?' He took the jacket from Bel, barely noticing the weight of hit in his hand.

Had they succeeded in moving a soul from the ethereal domain of Kur to this Earthly plane? A great part of the task their god-soldier lives were devoted to.

Bel did not look at him as the maladroit moment stretched out. All at once, Eron was achingly tired. Too tired to stand there like a desperate animal waiting for a scrap. So he walked away. Making an unsteady line for the door, he'd almost reached it when Bel finally answered.

'It was a success,' Bel said. 'The First Meld was a success. The goddess succeeded in releasing a gallu from Kur, and the carapace entombing him appears structurally sound.'

His sensory endings tingled with the revelation, and Eron dared another question. 'And Ereshkigal's Messenger, the boy, he survived?'

Tamas Cressly. The Facility's owner, inheriting the place at the death of his mother several years earlier. Tamas's mother had spent a better part of her life doing the goddess's bidding, only to die as most did, unremarkably. Her body consumed by its own treachery. Cancer at her breast. The family descended from a powerful lineage, the Abgal Utuabzu, seven sages created by the greater gods themselves and sent to instruct the humans thousands of years ago. Messengers. A bloodline so rare now the boy was considered to be the very last with any true strength. The last of the pure Messengers:

human conduits, living bridges between the divine and the human. But the bloodline did not grant immortality. That was reserved for the gods alone.

'He survived,' Bel said. 'Drained, as one might expect from such an effort, but he lives.'

Eron stood in perfect stillness, his hand raised over the sensor which would release the doors. Quite possibly, Tamas was the only one in the Facility who felt worse than he did.

'I understand.'

The hush of the opening doors swallowed his words, and he could not be sure Bel had heard them at all. Eron stepped into the main corridor, and the doors closed behind him. The First Meld was a success, and Eron had not been a witness to it. The bitterness of it swept through his dual stomachs. A creature of Kur had been raised into this world, sent by the goddess Herself, and his shortcomings had deprived him of witnessing the very reason for being on this world at all. Eron pinched the tatto, dug his fingernails into his skin, willing it to hurt. There was nothing.

Eron spoke to no one as he made his way back up to level eight, to his own quiet room. There was no one in his elevator for the short journey, and when he stepped out onto the silver-carpeted foyer of level eight, the security guards there gave him a nod but said nothing. Which suited Eron just fine.

He made his way to his room, furthest down the arched corridor. The walls were painted in the starkest white, and framed paintings of landscapes, various locations around Earth, had been hung along them. The air-conditioning unit hummed around him, pushing out filtered air, never altering from its steady pattern. Entering his room, he pulled off his jacket and threw it onto the apparently expensive but incredibly uncomfortable leather couch that took up most of the space in the main room. He had two intentions. Shower. Sleep.

He stripped off the rest of his clothes and stepped into the cubicle. Jets of hot water rushed at him from vertical and horizontal angles. If he were honest with himself, he'd admit he was not sorry to be missing service. Exclusion from that daily session of worship was the least vexing of his punishments. But being honest with himself had not served him well of late.

Eron watched his slow-to-colour skin move to a soft pink shade beneath the water's heat, his thoughts drifting to the First Meld. It must have been a magnificent sight, after thousands of years of absence, the gods stirring once again on this miniscule, lonely world. He stared at the droplets of water streaming around the stone embedded in his forearm. No moisture clung to the mea stone, repelled by the power of the relic. A power that would have coursed freely at the First Meld. Igniting the energy of the stones each of them bore.

Eron stepped out of the shower, wiped a hand across the condensation on the mirror. His snow-white hair hung limp on either side of his face. A faint trace of veins was visible beneath his skin, a sure sign of fatigue. The pale blue of his irises was dull beneath the thin layer of white that covered the entirety of his eyes. Humans were unsettled by two things. Firstly, that he and his soldier-brothers skirted a fine line between the masculine and feminine of the human race. Androgynous, Kira had explained after he'd asked her why one of the guards insisted on knowing if he was endowed with a cunt or a cock. Humans were ill-equipped to deal with the lack of either, it seemed, and so the Syranians had been dubbed male, and were referred to as 'he' and 'him'. Bestowed with honorary cocks. Secondly, humans appeared to abhor the Syranians' eyes. Eron's eyeballs looked to be entirely white unless one drew close enough to see the hint of colour beneath. People's demeanours changed the instant he wore contact lenses. Suddenly, Eron and his brothers became less alien. Less threatening.

A melodic shrill notified him of someone requesting access to his room. Eron strode naked back out into the main room. He brushed his fingers through the delicate fronds of one of the many plants dotting the living space before reaching the door's video feed. The woman who waited outside his room was vaguely familiar: short-cropped black hair full of wiry tight curls, deep brown skin, and wearing a crumpled white jacket that marked her as a laboratory worker. He scanned her ID tag: Gwen Weylen. Biomechanic.

Clearly a lab worker with full security clearance if she was here, on this level. Talking to him.

'Eron here.' He released the communicator, careful not to allow reverse visual access.

'Mr Eron, sir.' Gwen's gaze was a darting, wild thing moving from the camera lens to scan the hallway she stood in. 'Mr Eron, sir, I was wondering if you could come with me.'

Eron glanced down at his naked self. 'Why would I do that?'

'I know we haven't met directly before, but Blake has sent me.'

Blake Beckworth, or as he and his kind called her, the Technician. Kira's sister. For an inopportune moment Eron's voice failed him. He swallowed, tried again. 'I'm sorry?'

'Blake.' Gwen leaned in towards the camera. 'Blake asked me to come and get you. She needs your help.'

'Help?'

'Assistance.' Gwen scratched at her temple with the corner of her ID. 'She needs your assistance, just briefly. Seeing as the others are unavailable. The other –'

Aliens. Yes, he understood. Except he didn't. Blake Beckworth had barely exchanged more than a handful of words with him over the years. Nothing personal – the girl spared little conversation for anyone. Including her own sister.

'I will need to clarify this with –'

'Your captain has given approval, Eron, sir.' Gwen's voice did an odd little jump. 'You're good to go. But we should leave now.'

The captain's approval. Perhaps Lahar had listened to his prayers after all.

'I'll be with you in just a moment.'

TAMAS - 3

Tamas Cressly eased his legs over the side of his king bed and stopped to catch his breath. Tinnitus hissed in his eardrums, and something in the room smelled foul. Gingerly sniffing his cupped hand, Tamas discovered the source of the odour. Vomit. His raw, burned throat confirmed it, and a glance down at his clothes revealed he no longer wore the white linen shirt he'd donned for the First Meld. It had been replaced with a black cotton T-shirt. Which meant someone had undressed him and cleaned him. Touched his skin. A river of goosebumps pierced their way through his warm body, and his empty stomach threatened to find something else to release. He glanced around the room, blinking against the morning light streaming through the windows, catching a blurry glimpse of the shoulder-high reeds in the garden outside. A replica of the marshlands of his homeland. War had destroyed most of the original beauty in Iraq, and it had taken his father's life, too. But here, in the middle of a very different desert thousands of kilometres from the aggression, the natural beauty had thrived in the garden his mother had designed. It was six years since her death, and he still wasted copious amounts of water keeping the replica alive.

Not for her. For the garden. A place that always managed to soothe him. As did the realisation now that he was utterly alone. Whoever had played nursemaid was gone. Better still, the goddess was absent from her usual place in his head. Tamas sighed and touched his toes to the floor. The maroon tiles were refreshingly cool against skin that still burned from the night's activity. His entire body ached with the remnants of the Meld's force. The skin beneath his precisely shaven beard itched ferociously, and something caked his eyelashes like a layer of sand . Suffice to say, he probably looked as good as he felt, and that was not great at all. He pulled off the black shirt, grabbed a floral-print favourite that should have been laundered a few days ago, and tugged on a pair of jeans that lay in a faded blue lump beside the bed. He pressed his fingers to his lips and wondered if his ancestors, the ones who had received a Calling, had felt this rotten each time the gods moved through them. If breast cancer hadn't taken his mother, she would have been the one bearing the burden. And she wouldn't have been standing here feeling sorry for herself. She would have gloated and pranced and preened as if she were the goddess herself, looking down her nose, as she so often did, at Tamas. But she was a pile of ash sprinkled in the Tier, taking all her rage, knowledge, and self-importance with her. Did she see him? He often wondered. Did she feel any sense of pride that a son she'd branded useless for the most part was now Ereshkigal's Messenger in her place?

He smiled at the mirror as he brushed his teeth. Spit, rinse, and a splash to the face. The burst of icy water cleared the fogginess a little. Tamas ran impatient fingers through his short dark hair, slapped on deodorant, and left his room, stepping out into the brightness of the glass corridor that linked his private quarters to the access elevator. It had one of the best views in the Facility, floor-to-ceiling glass panels that afforded a view uninterrupted even by the security fencing ringing the complex. Tamas's room looked out across the desert, towards the low-level mountain range that curved around the backside of the Facility. Everything was dusty pink. Even the deep olive tone of his skin had dustings of the sun's blush upon it. He pressed the call button on the elevator and crouched on his haunches, back pressed hard against the white marble wall. No expense spared. His mother's taste had bordered on outlandish, and the income brought in by the Facility's sought-after tech, predominantly Blake's designs, had only fed her appetite.

Despite having just woken, Tamas's body weighed him down. He wanted to rest. For a very, very long time. His blurred reflection regarded him in the glass panel work of the elevator doors: the dark mop of his hair, the smudge of stubble on his chin and cheeks. Movement at the far end of the hallway caught his attention. Someone stepped into his space. Granted, it was a lot of space. The length of the hallway stood between him and the man; at least a dozen paces separated them. But the way Tamas's heart rate quickened and skin warmed with a blush, the man might as well have been holding a knife to his throat. Catching sight of Tamas, he raised a hand, a smile lifting his lips, adding further wrinkles to an already well-burdened face.

'Oh, hey there, young man. I've gotten myself a little lost. There should be a conference room round here somewhere, I believe.'

Tamas's mouth was parched as dry as the desert surrounding the Facility, and the dampness of sweat oozed beneath his armpits. Whoever this fool was, he was not only lost, he was oblivious too, with no clue to whom he spoke.

His boss.

One who didn't like strangers. Didn't like the way coming across an unknown person rendered him a speechless, trembling mess. Tamas pushed so hard against the wall his vertebrae felt fit to crack under the pressure. His breath escaped him in quick, sharp puffs. The man waited on a reply, went so far as to take a step down the hall towards Tamas.

'Are you okay?' he said, pulling a cleaning cart into the corridor behind him. Brooms and mops and other paraphernalia jutted out of it, like oversized porcupine quills. Just a cleaner. The guy was amongst the lowest paid of any on the Facility grounds, yet here Tamas was, huddling like a frightened child, willing the damn elevator to open and swallow him whole. Tamas forced a slow breath, digging his fingers into the woodwork beneath him.

'Go . . .' Only one croaky syllable escaped him.

But a reprieve came from elsewhere. A woman suddenly appeared behind the man, and her eyes widened at the sight of Tamas. She grabbed the man, the material of his sleeve bunching in her fist, and hauled him back into the corridor they'd stepped from.

'My apologies, Mr Cressly. Samson is new.' She stumbled over her own words, and over Samson, as she backpedalled them out of sight. Tamas caught the woman's words as the pair hurried down the echoing walkway.

'Idiot. That's the boss. What the hell were you thinking?'

'That boy? He doesn't look old enough to –'

'He's old enough to sign your paychecks, and he doesn't like to be disturbed. Ever. Don't you ever . . .'

What the cleaner should never do was lost to Tamas as the couple moved out of earshot, leaving only tinnitus to disturb his peace. The elevator door eased open. Wiping sweaty palms against his jeans, Tamas jerked to his feet and stepped inside. By the time he reached level eleven, the anxiety attack was an embarrassing memory, added to the pile of embarrassing memories stored up over the years. It would not always be this way. Serve the goddess well and great things would come his way. He would be the one who caused people to tremble and stammer. Not the other way around.

Tamas stepped out of the reassuringly small confines of the elevator and into the corridor. The land the Facility was built on, and into, had once been a salt mine. After that, it had been a government facility, a testing base for secret initiatives, both airborne and biological, before being closed down. A few years later Tamas's mum had decided the abandoned complex was where they would wait. Prescience, a gift from the goddess that so far Tamas had not been privy to, led his mother from their homeland of Iraq to here, the United States, a few years after Tamas had been born. Not to this particular place, in the middle of the desert, but she was too ambitious, too restless not to do something while they waited on the goddess's next divine instruction. A human could waste a lifetime waiting on a deity who operated on an entirely different timescale. Tamas's grandfather had, apparently. The man had been something of a monster to his mother as year after year passed and he did not receive a Calling. Probably explained why she was so good at being a bitch herself. Years of training. But she had been a damn good robotics engineer and had decided to continue a career begun in Iraq. She'd purchased the ruined complex and turned it into a formidable robotics and engineering facility, giving Tamas next to no choice on his own career path. He pressed his fingers against his temples, seeking to ease the tightness building in his skull.

'Please, not yet. Just a little longer,' he muttered to the empty elevator.

Tamas had always been curious about how much Ereshkigal had influenced his mother's interests and drive. Had the goddess injected her with some kind of natural attraction to this work? Because it had become a very fortuitous choice of career, as well as venue. The Facility, perched and isolated in the desert, filled with top-secret projects – some military, some private – was the perfect place to hide the extraterrestrial visitors his mother had been told by the goddess to expect. Tamas tapped his finger against the wall. As much as he yearned for the answer, there was no way he'd ever try to satisfy his curiosity. Ereshkigal wasn't exactly the high authority on small talk.

Level eleven's sole corridor was one of the complex's original tunnels, a massive, arching passageway where white rock was still exposed and the floor had not been covered in concrete like most of the rest. Tamas knew every dip and rise in the packed-earth beneath him. The air always held a heaviness down here, cool but not unpleasant, blanketing the space around him and muffling the sounds of his footsteps. The glow from the strip lighting along the floor didn't reach all the way to the domed roof, leaving it in shadow. He passed through the spiderweb-like laser pattern that spread from one side of the passageway to the other. The security system acknowledged and accepted the presence of the Facility director, and he continued on. A bolt of pain seared through his right temple, and Tamas braced one hand against the rough wall. The goddess did not intend for him to see the results of last evening alone. She was coming. The prickling of his nerves and the heightening hiss of the tinnitus told him that.

His mother had relished the pain of a Calling the way Benedictine monks once embraced self-flagellation The more it hurt, the better. Tamas did not share her zeal. With Ereshkigal's last visit so recent, her return was bitingly sharp.

Before long, the solid mass of steel-reinforced concrete which marked the entrance to the main chamber of level eleven came into view. Two people stood guard at the entranceway, both clad in forest-green uniforms starched to within an inch of their lives. The last of Tamas's tension left him. He knew the guards, ex-soldiers employed by his mother. Tamas approached them, his cheeks as cool as the tunnel air, his heartbeat steady. He'd known the two people in front of him, a dark-skinned man named Reuben and a Korean-born woman called Nari, long enough that his anxiety had nothing to feed on here.

'Good morning . . . ah, good morning to you both.'

His voice was a little husky, but there it was. Proof that he was not always the bumbling idiot he'd been reduced to in his own hallway. Nari betrayed nothing, keeping her eyes on the ground. Reuben regarded Tamas for all of a heartbeat. 'Good morning to you, sir.'

The guard gave Tamas a deep nod, then pushed in the access code, opening a smaller door set within the greater panel that blocked off the passageway. The door swung open, and Tamas felt the prickling air rush out at him from the chamber, brushing against him like static electricity. Tamas curled his shaking hands into fists, straightened his shoulders, and stepped into the hollow enormity of the level eleven chamber. The goddess smashed into the back of his skull the way a rabid animal might throw itself against its cage. He stumbled, but caught himself before anyone might consider coming to his aid. Taking deep breaths, he paused. Gathering himself. Concentrating on the physical world around him while he waited for Her to settle.

The chamber was a huge naturally formed cavern, one that had been here since before the time of the ancient Sumerians, the very first peoples to worship Ereshkigal Herself. As in the passageway, there had been no attempts to conceal the natural rock here, something Tamas thought made it all the more magnificent. Awesome stalagmites rose from the floor at various intervals, some as thick as oak tree trunks, others no more than saplings. Stalactites dotted the cavern roof like hovering swords. These formations were not strictly natural occurrences. They had appeared in a matter of months, not thousands of years. Beginning to grow from the moment the Syranians emptied their payload of Waters into the man-made pool at the heart of the huge space five years ago.

The largest cluster of stalactites hung directly over the well at the centre of the chamber. Tamas hesitated. Even from this distance, a good twenty metres, the pull of the Waters lapped at him. The liquid lay dark and utterly still in a circular containment area, about half the size and depth of the average swimming pool.

Last night, Tamas had stepped into those Waters and provided Ereshkigal with the fragile connection she needed to guide a gallu from her realm of Kur into the corporeal world of the humans. In the times of the ancient Sumerians, when the bridge between Kur and Earth still stood strong, the people had called the preternatural creatures demons and devils. It was a generalisation that was unkind to at least some of the gallu but he could vouch that it was hellish enough to bring one of them here. Even now the residual energy from the Meld rubbed like sandpaper against Tamas's synapses.

Someone waved to him from across the chamber, catching his attention. Tamas returned Blake's greeting. She stood a few metres in front of the largest of three modular rooms that had been built up against the rock, jutting out like three giant shoeboxes from the jagged rock face. Tamas headed towards her, making his way around his favourite stalagmite formation, running his fingertips over the bumps and bulges of it. She met him halfway. The Syranians called her the Technician. The somewhat cold moniker suited her.

'Blake,' he said. 'Have you been here all night?'

The rings under her eyes appeared painted on. Her black hair, deep as night, hung against her pale skin.

'Yes, I have,' she said. 'I thought you were going to die last night.'

Tamas laughed. The movement hurt his ribcage, but he couldn't help himself. Blake's bluntness was reliably amusing. His voice never cracked with her, his cheeks didn't bloom red.

'I thought I might too, for a little while. But,' he gestured towards himself, 'I survived.'

She didn't reply, just stared at him, her amber eyes never leaving his. He recognised the distant look she wore because she wore it so often. Even more so over the past few weeks. Tamas waited, staring back at her. There was a cluster of veins at her right temple he didn't remember seeing before. Blake's cheekbones were too defined. She forgot to eat far too often. Tamas made a mental note to speak with Rossiter and have him monitor her consumption.

The goddess, apparently not fond of silence, roared into his mind with a force that staggered him.

'Are you sick?' Blake's nose lifted, ever so slightly.

'Blake, can you take me to him?' He touched a finger to his temple. 'I didn't quite make it till the end of proceedings, as you know, and the goddess isn't too happy.'

Blake's distant expression snapped away, replaced with the guarded mask she always wore when the gods were mentioned. 'I won't be withdrawing the inhibitors till the captain is done with service. The proper protocols need to be in place. Does your boss understand?'

The goddess's reply roared like a brain freeze through Tamas's skull. He held his breath, determined not to let the discomfort show. Ereshkigal was not pleased. Mostly at Blake's impressively stubborn refusal to believe the goddess existed at all.

'That's fine.'

'We should keep this brief,' Blake said. 'You need to rest.'

It was kind of impressive, the degree of scepticism Blake still maintained. She never called Ereshkigal by name, never mentioned gods and goddesses. To Blake the gods were some other alien species, ultimately knowable and understandable.

Tamas walked behind her, eyes down to avoid unnecessary eye contact with the smattering of personnel at work in the chamber. He kept his gaze on Blake's purple steel-toed boots, a present from Kira a few Christmas's ago. Blake had barely gone a day without wearing them since. After watching the sisters' complicated relationship for so long, he was kind of grateful he had no siblings. Tamas lifted his head as they reached the steps to Tech Room One. The brighter light inside the room wasn't kind against his raw senses. He squinted, focusing on what lay at the room's centre. The buck of recognition coming from the deity inside his head caused him to sway. Tamas steadied himself against the door.

A man lay prone on a white porcelain examination table. He was surrounded by monitoring equipment, which hummed and beeped with electronic declarations. Here lay the result of the First Meld. The first of five gallu to be sent by the goddess from Kur. This creature was only a guinea pig; he would not be a hunter as the other Four would. He would not be a part of the search for Dumuzi, the demigod long buried inside the living, breathing flesh suit of a human. This gallu was to test the carapaces and enable the Syranians to train for what was to come.

'The design is holding?' he said, not taking his eyes from the slow rise and fall of the man's chest. There was no real intake of oxygen involved. The movement was all for show.

'Yes, it is.' Blake stood alongside him, close enough that the fabric of their sleeves touched. There'd been a time when they had been even closer. A one-off that neither wished to repeat. Discovering that what they really desired were the long comfortable silences and the acceptance of the fact that they were willing slaves to their work. Blake didn't give a toss if he stuttered; she barely listened to him at all. 'What do you think? Is this what they wanted?'

'I believe so.'

The Technician's work was flawless. Tamas had watched Blake build every part of the shell that lay before them now. From the very first sketches of the metallic skeleton, to the development of the tools needed to work with the Syranian metal Telteriun, to the development of the faux skin that bound it all together. This human carapace was a constructed masterpiece, but for all intents and purposes, a cage. The gallu had to be restrained in order to be controlled. And control would be needed when they would be used like hunting dogs to find Dumuzi.

The artificial man looked to be in his late twenties. His upper body was bare, his lower body clad in green linen pants that didn't quite cover the sharp V-shaped muscles running from his hips towards his pelvis. His skin was a deep olive, much darker than Tamas's own, with a square defined jaw and chin; dark, heavy brow and strong flared nose. The man was average height – the Syranians would tower over him – but his body was taut, with a hint of muscular tone that suggested greater underlying strength. Blake had literally taken him from the cover of a magazine, several magazines, creating a mash-up of two Iraqi models she'd discovered online. Her creation was a living Photoshop image. Impossible perfection. A reflection of that brief moment at the beginning of all this when Blake had been dazzled by the divinity around her.

But Tamas had seen the other carapaces. Her beguilement had long since passed.

'You're not saying anything,' Blake said, adjusting the circlet around the man's head which fed back vital-sign data. 'What does she think of Azrael?'

'Azrael?' Tamas stood slightly back from the table. He'd thought the Syranian metal would contain the gallu's energy entirely, but the punch to his senses told him otherwise. Between that and the wild, darting sensations the goddess sent through him, Tamas's skin felt fit to burst.

'You said it didn't have a name, the thing she sent through.' Blake ran fingertips across the crown of her head, doing little to tidy the uncharacteristically untidy ponytail she'd bound her jet-black hair in. 'I figured your boss wouldn't mind if I named it.'

'Named it after the angel of death?'

Blake shrugged. 'It seems as good a name as any. These things are coming here to kill someone, aren't they?'

A catch in her voice caught his attention. Since the days of university when they'd studied together, he'd only ever seen Blake's emotions swamp her once – the day she'd stared down at Kira's broken body, fresh from the wreck that had taken their father. As she'd watched her sister's life ebb away with the blood they couldn't stop pouring from her busted organs, Blake had shed a couple of tears, but minutes later she'd been unreadable again. Everything had been locked away.

'Well, yes. But not this one.' He wanted to say something that would clear the darkness from her face. 'Not Azrael. He's a test run, a prototype. And just think of where this tech will —'

'Tamas, it's okay. A deal's a deal, and I'm holding up my end.' Blake pulled the folds of her too-large blouse tighter around her. 'I simply need some processing time after last night. So if your boss is done, I'd like to tidy up here and get some sleep before the next stage.'

Tamas's answer was decided by the arrival of a lab tech, a young woman with short-cropped red hair and full cheeks. She knew better than the cleaner. She didn't say a word to Tamas, just gave a slight nod to acknowledge him, and then she moved to the back of the tech room, busying herself with a laptop at a standing desk. Blake ushered Tamas outside, leaving no doubt that his time was up. She spoke to him as she walked him out into the chamber, but Tamas could barely make out the words through the shocking rush of tinnitus filling his skull. The goddess, his boss, was indeed done. Ereshkigal slipped from that place she coveted in his mind, just as Blake turned and left him. Neither spared a thought for the flesh-and-blood man stumbling his way across the empty cavern. Now-vacant head filled with thoughts of a time that would come when he would not be so invisible.

KIRA - 4

Kira stepped out of the service elevator behind Rossiter and dry-retched. A giant industrial bin stood to their left, lid up, cavernous innards empty.

'Fuck me, that stinks.' Kira placed a palm over her mouth and tasted sambuca against her skin. 'Oh Jesus, I need a shower.' She tried to run her fingers through her mop of curls, but one knuckle deep, the journey was thwarted by giant knots. 'Shit, balls, shit.'

Rossiter waved a giant paw at her. 'Keep it down.'

There was nothing Kira loved more than being shushed after no sleep and with veins still full of booze. She opened her mouth, ready with a few choice morsels, but caught sight of the main chamber of level eleven through the narrow glass panes on the door ahead. The words slid back down her throat. Her sister stood with Tamas by the world's lamest spa. Some mouldy old well that was supposedly super important, full of rare extraterrestrial water. Or some crap. Her guts leapfrogged as she watched Blake. The weirdest thought of running to her and giving her a hug crossed Kira's mind. Yeah, right. That would go down like a lead balloon. There had been no hugs since . . . oh fuck it. Hugging was a bad idea. Kira could count on one hand how many times she'd been down here. One hand too many. It was just wrong to be this far underground, this was a domain for burrowing creatures, groundhogs, or whatever things burrowed. Not humans. Fitting, she supposed, considering down here was all about aliens.

'She looks like shit.' It wasn't a whisper, but it was as close as Kira could be bothered to get. 'So does Tamas. Seriously, those two need to get out into daylight more often. Oh my god, is that what she's going to tell me? Blake's a vampire? I knew my sister was a freak.'

She punctuated her words with a slap of her hand against Rossiter's shoulder. Might as well have slapped a mountain. He glowered at her, narrowing his dark eyes to the barest slits, and pressed a finger against his lips. Seriously, why the hell had she been summoned down here if she was supposed to hide out with the garbage? There were much better things, and people, to be doing on a Saturday morning. Speaking of which, the bulge in Rossiter's pants was mesmerising. Sure, she'd never go there, 'cause yuck, but that didn't mean it wasn't impressive. Didn't steroids usually kill that kind of hardware?

'My eyes are up here,' Rossiter hissed. 'Focus, will you? Try to at least act sober.'

Behind them, the elevator doors closed with the barest brush of sound. There was a clunk and a whir, and the elevator drifted upwards. Kira swallowed hard, trying to block out the sound as it grew more distant. They were a long way down, and right now, there was no immediate escape. It pissed her off, the way that thought made her fingers shake. Although, it could have been the line she'd shared with Liam that made her tremble like a jellyfish, not the enormous amount of dirt and rock that stood between her and sky.

'Lead the way, giant man.' Kira swept her metal arm in a flourish, and the oversized buckles on Perry's vinyl jacket clinked with the movement.

'I told you, we're waiting till Tamas leaves. Blake doesn't want anyone to know she's brought you down here. We weren't expecting him, not after…' Rossiter's words dissolved in the air as his fingertips tapped out an uneven beat against the brickwork. Kira considered asking him what the 'not after' referred to, but decided that on the scale of one to ten fucks given, she was sitting at a one. The answer would involve some engineering and technical boring-as-bat-shit lingo that would reduce her to tears with its inanity, and she didn't feel like crying.

'What a pity. Tamas is like my best buddy.' Kira sighed. 'I'd love to say hi.'

Rossiter ignored her, eyes fixed on the two people at the centre of the enormous cavern. Most of the Facility knew exactly what Kira thought of Tamas. That he was a dick. A dickless dick. Perry had said once that jealousy might be at the core of it. That Blake spent more time and shared more secrets with the insipid little shit than she did her own sister, and Kira didn't like it. She'd rewarded Perry's deduction by stealing his car and disappearing for twenty-four hours. He'd been well pissed. Obviously, he loved his Audi more than she'd realised.

'Holy shit.' Kira jumped at a thought. 'Is Tamas a vampire too?'

But Rossiter had reached what she liked to refer to as his 'K-threshold'. When he was done with her shit, he went silent. Didn't bite when she tried to throw a line. No way in hell would she ever tell him, but Kira kind of liked the impenetrable wall of silence he put up. Her gaze moved back to her sister. Blake had escaped the curly-hair curse, and her perfectly straight shoulder-length black hair was in its usual ponytail. But usually it was pulled back so hard she wouldn't need a facelift for years to come. Today it looked as though field mice had held an MMA match in the strands. And if Blake lost any more weight, there would be no skin to tuck back in a facelift. The long-sleeved pastel-green shirt and ill-fitting black pants seemed to be the only thing holding Blake's skeleton together. Fuck, she was gaunt. Gaunt. Man, that word needed to be used more, Kira decided.

Finally, Tamas turned to leave. He had his arms wrapped round his belly, as though he felt like Kira did right now, not trusting her stomach contents to stay where they were. He was thirty-something, but he was moving as if he were ready for a Zimmer frame. Kira made a mental note to buy one and have it put in his room. Hilarious.

'Right. You're sorted then.' Rossiter moved back over to the elevator. 'I'll leave you two to have your usual pleasant conversations.'

A moment later the twin silver doors of the elevator slid back. It wasn't empty. The occupant stared directly at Kira. Her breath jammed into the back of her throat, just as it did every time she saw the guy. It had been a while.

Kira lifted her hand, flicked out a lazy wave. 'Eron, hey, how's the banishment going? They still got you in the naughty corner?' *Treat 'em mean, keep 'em keen* had always worked well.

Eron's expression didn't shift from a sulky supermodel

pout of disinterest as he stepped from the elevator.

'I'm sure you are aware of the circumstances. I was not permitted to attend the First Meld last night,' he said, his alien accent lacing his English with a vaguely Eastern European lilt.

'Totes. Must have sucked, not . . . melding.' Kira shrugged.

What in all hells was a First Meld? And who the fuck cared? Unless it was some ET orgy, in which case where the fuck had her invitation gone? Least they could do was reward her for keeping the BIG secret all these years. No easy task keeping quiet about the aliens in the basement when ethanol was pretty much your best friend.

Christ, he was beautiful. Lips too full, and curves tracing a salivating, and confusing, line between the hardness of a dude's features and the fleshier, more tantalising delicacy of a woman's. All the aliens had the androgynous thing going on, but none of them skirted the feminine line quite like Eron did. If her heart hadn't been a chunk of machinery, and it could actually beat, it would have thumped like a friggin' pole driver right then. Kira forced herself to take a breath. Get a grip. Control the little monster between her legs.

Eron nodded to Rossiter, who in turn nodded back, muttering something about them not wasting time in here and getting to Blake.

'I'm heading back to surveillance. Keep an eye on things,' Rossiter said, but no one paid him any mind.

The elevator doors closed and they were alone. Eron's gaze rested on her. His face was framed by his long silver-white hair. From this distance his eyes were two orbs of complete white. But she knew that close up, very close up, there was the barest hint of blue beneath the snow. The hue always shone just a little brighter when her fingers found a particular spot, right up high on his inner thigh. Things got a little warmer in her panties and Kira turned away. So much for getting a grip. What in all the holy bejesuses was Blake up to?

The door separating them from the main chamber slid open. Blake stood there, all five foot three undernourished inches of her. A button was missing about halfway up her pastel-green shirt, hinting at a flesh-coloured bra beneath. Tweezers were desperately needed to launch a plucking attack on her dark eyebrows. Kira chewed at the dry skin on her bottom lip. She'd not seen Blake in a month. B had never been a clothes horse, never even worn mascara, but boy, she'd let things slide in a big way.

Blake glanced at Kira, her gaze darting up and down, but her expression gave nothing away. She turned to Eron.

'We need to make this brief. Come with me.'

'Hey, sis, missed you too. No hugs?' Kira raised her

arms and pursed her lips. 'Maybe a smooch?'

'I don't have time for your childishness, Kira —'

'Saying hello is childish now? Wow, things changed a lot while I was in Bali.'

'Just hurry up, Kira. Eron, this way.'

Blake turned and strode away, purple boots barely making a sound on the packed-earth floor. Despite the money they had to throw at things, Tamas wanted the cavern kept as close to natural as possible. And whatever Tamas wanted, he got. The guy couldn't look Kira in the eye without his face blooming deep red, but he had Blake and most of the Facility wrapped round his little finger. Amazing what cash did to a person's popularity. Kira could vouch for that. Jogging to keep up, she fell in behind Eron, enjoying the view.

'I fail to understand the necessity for my presence here, Technician,' Eron said.

Kira wrinkled her nose. The nickname the aliens had given Blake was so fucking lame. It made Blake sound like some kind of rogue dentist. A rogue dentist who could walk superfast when she wanted to. Blake easily outpaced them across the chamber and ignored Eron's question. He strode after Blake in slo-mo like an admonished toddler who doesn't want to follow too close after mummy when she tells him to hurry up. He kept darting glances at the main door of the chamber. And at her. She could see the looks from where she hid behind her knotted shock of black hair. But he wasn't exactly making goggly-eyes at her. When something irritated Eron, he would push his long silver locks behind his ears, over and over, despite the fact that they hadn't come loose. His fingers were in overdrive right now.

'All good there, big guy?' Kira came out from her little hairy hidey-hole and drew alongside him. The guy actually flinched, shuffled away. Nice. How to make a girl feel good about herself. Ass.

'I don't understand why I am here,' he said.

'You and me both, gorgeous.'

Eron shrugged his narrow shoulders and fluttered fingertips to his lips. As if she were leaving a bad taste in his mouth. Jesus, they'd fucked around, not gotten married. Kira moved away, pulling Perry's jacket tighter around her. Fair enough though really. Being put on lockdown by his uptight captain as punishment for sneaking off-site and playing with human pussy must have sucked. Captain Nex had kept Eron underground for over a month. After her happy time with Eron had become common knowledge amongst the other aliens, some of the looks cast her way could have killed her more dead than she'd been on the operating table three years ago.

The thud of Blake's boots reverberated around the cavern. The near-deserted cavern.

Maybe that was why Blake had chosen this time to get her down here, while Captain Nex and his buddies were in their pray-pray session. Kira glanced around the chamber. There was a definite lack of any other living beings in the cavern. Or nonliving, for that matter. No trace of even one of the shit-scary metal cats usually lurking around here. Creepy fucking things. Robots with bodies like silver cheetahs, but headless. Who designs something like that? Fucked-up nerds, that's who. Tamas and Blake had designed them a few years back for security, supposedly. So where was all the precious security now?

'Okay.' Kira stopped dead, the alcohol leaving her system far faster than she would have liked. 'Back the truck up, sis. This load ain't leaving till you spill. What the hell is going on?'

ERON - 5

The crispness in the air, the hum of last night's energy, laced every breath Eron took. The very particles of oxygen were alive with it. Eron stared hard at Blake's back – as much to show his disapproval at the summons as to give himself something to focus on other than Kira. 'I believe that is not an altogether unreasonable question, Miss Beckworth. As I said, I do not see the necessity for my presence here.'

The elder Beckworth sister did not halt her rapid journey across the chamber, despite Kira's demand for explanation. 'I brought you here to provide safety, Eron,' Blake said. 'Your presence is a precaution only. And as you are currently out of favour, I'm counting on your discretion.'

A distinctly unpleasant doubt now wound its way through Eron's mind. He had not questioned the biotechnician Gwen Weylen's assurances that this visit had been approved by

Captain Nex.

'Seriously, Blake,' Kira called, 'I'm not following you. You're acting even weirder than normal, and that's too much weird for me.'

Eron's smile reached his lips unbidden. He quickly tilted his head, ensuring Kira did not notice his amusement. It would not do to give her any opportunity to engage with him too deeply. When she drew too close, her presence released an unpredictability within him that Eron abhorred. He focused on the departing Technician. Cym, the Syranian medic, had expressed some concern about her health, and it was not difficult to understand why. The woman showed definite signs of undernourishment. But it did not hinder her pace. The Beckworths were not graced with height, yet Blake's short legs were carrying her at a formidable speed across the chamber. In four more strides she would reach the first of three rectangular rooms which jutted out from the far wall of the cavern. The central room was the largest, and she was clearly headed for its unimposing door. Each room had a rather lack-lustre name: Tech Room One, Two, or Three.

'I must ask that you divulge your plans, Miss Beckworth. I cannot be a part of –' Eron flicked a sideways glance. Kira had abandoned her stance on staying still, and walked far too close. He should not even be in her vicinity, let alone alongside her.

But all he could focus on was the jacket she wore. Obviously not her own.

'Step one of the entire reason your people are here at all lies in that room over there.' Blake pointed to the central tech room. 'Azrael arrived last night. And no matter how much you bluster about protocol, I know you won't leave, Eron. I know you want to see him. So let's not waste any more time on that.'

Now it was Eron's turn to stop. He drew back his shoulders. 'Azrael?'

'He needed a name. No one seemed to know or care what his real one was.' Blake turned to face him. 'So I gave him one.' Green-grey veins formed in a small cluster at her temples. She held a distant look, one she was well practised in. Her inability to focus on general conversation was a trait Eron knew drove Kira to distraction. Eron dug his fingertips into his thighs. 'I see.' Though he did not, not really.

It was superfluous to give the creature a name. Ereshkigal sent them a lesser being for the First Meld, a soul of no import in her realm. One that would not be missed should there be any catastrophic failure of the carapace, which was a viable and probable result. The gallu of Kur could not long survive in this godless corporeal world without a shielding. The metal shells constructed by Cym and the Technician— made of Telteriun and blessed by Lahar, one of the last Living Gods—were not unlike those worn by human astronauts; life preservers capable of sustaining life in an environment otherwise uninhabitable. Even the Four – by far the most powerful of all the gallu – would suffer if unshielded on Earth, and without the carapaces would soon have to abandon this world if they intended to survive. The First Meld was a test run designed to reveal any flaws.

'Right, well I don't see shit,' Kira said. 'Who the fuck is Azrael? And has he brought booze with him?' She scratched at her head, and the movement shifted her jacket open, exposing her hole-ridden shirt. A sudden lightheadedness gripped Eron. He'd removed that shirt from her body once, the red bra beneath, too. The air grew heated, and Eron adjusted the top buckle on his vest.

'I need you sober.' Blake glared at Kira. 'I need you to pay attention.'

'Pay attention to what, dear sister? It's been so long since you called I thought maybe you'd died down here. That would have made two of us.'

Kira smiled at her own humour. The curve to her lips created a dimple in her left cheek, but the memory of the day of the accident brought no mirth for Eron. He recalled the cool and detached way the captain had declared the death of Blake's father a serendipitous event, and Kira's horrific injuries an opportunity. The eager way Tamas had agreed. One way to stem Blake's increasing concerns about the Syranians' true intentions – despite her obsession with their technology and her own lust for knowledge – was to make her irreversibly indebted to those she had begun to doubt. In truth, they needed her expertise. The captain and Cym were adept with advanced technology, but the nuances of humanity required a certain finesse.

And so, they had brought Blake's sister, her only surviving family member, back to her.

'Shut up, Kira.' Blake wiped at her brow. 'Are you sober enough to remember this?'

Blake stood at the top of the short flight of stairs leading into the tech room. She tilted her head to look down at her sister. Her large amber eyes were focused. She was present. And, if Eron wasn't reading her entirely wrong, there was a certain melancholy in her expression.

'Depends how memorable it's going to be,' Kira said. 'I mean is there going to be skinny dipping in that creepy-ass pool over there? That could be memorable.'

'Keep your clothes on, Kira. You are not in Tahiti now.'

There was a moment of silence. An unusual occurrence for Kira. Something about Blake's comment had caught her off guard.

'You saw that?' Kira said. 'That was a private fucking island. Who the hell got a photo? Jesus –'

Eron stared down at his booted feet again. While he had been restricted to the lower levels of the Facility, Kira had not even remained in the country. It should have angered him. Instead, Eron chased the image of her naked body out of his head.

'No one got a photo. It wasn't the press who knew you were there,' Blake said. 'I had you watched as a precaution. Now please, come on.'

Though Blake dismissed the conversation with a wave of her hand, Eron tensed at Kira's expression. When she frowned that way, closing up her left eye slightly more than the right, he knew that the intercourse would not be concluded anytime soon. Arguments enlivened her, she seemed to hunt them down and take a stranglehold on them. The sisters' disputes had been frequent and vocal in earlier days before Blake had distanced herself, and he did not lament their loss.

'Watched as a precaution? Blake, do you have any idea how fucked up it is that you don't see anything wrong with spying on me?' Kira's vehement lift of her arms seemed to throw her off balance. Eron crossed his own, determined not to reach and steady her.

'You're a mess, Kira.' Blake's melancholy had left her.

There was something hard there now.

'Well fuck you very much, but I'm not the one watching my sister have sex on a beach.'

Eron shifted on his feet. His inner voice was a solid chorus of sound, telling him to turn and leave. Now. But another part of him, that part that betrayed him so consistently, deadened the cacophony and rooted him to the spot.

'I didn't watch you,' Blake said. 'I have better things to do. I had information relayed.'

'Oh, that's okay then. Not. Jesus. Did Tamas authorise this? The dude needs to deal with some personal frustrations and use porn sites like everyone else.'

The pulse of tension bouncing between the sisters was a palpable thing. But where Kira made it physical in the clench of her fists, Blake held it all in her eyes. Eron felt as invisible now as any time during his solitude. He considered moving away, stepping closer to the Tier and letting its force replace this discomfort.

'Grow up, Kira. You gave us every reason to watch you.' Though she didn't look at him, Eron felt the jab of Blake's meaning.

'Holy crap, Blake, you couldn't just ask me where I was going? Or call me? I would have sent you photos if I'd known you gave a shit. But you've said three words to me in about a year, so I figured I was good.'

'I don't care about your photos.' Blake pressed her palm to the sensor, and the tech room door opened. Eron frowned, certain he'd noticed a trembling in her fingertips. 'I don't care about the beach you're on or the bikini you're not wearing. None of that matters. It is pathetic and trivial. I just wanted to know you were alive, that's all I needed. That's all I have time for.'

'Wow. Just, wow.' Kira shook her head. 'Those tactfulness classes are really working for you, aren't they? Sister of the year right there. Well you know what, I don't care about the new toys you're building down here. I don't care about your robot dogs or whatever other mechanical pieces of shit you're building. So I'm just going to go back up where the sun is shining and normal people are having normal fucking days.'

Blake turned away, but not before Eron caught the brittleness in her expression. She was exhausted, that was plain. 'Go. It was a mistake to ask you here.'

'Yep, probably was. Sound the bells, ring the alarms, Blake Beckworth made a mistake.' Kira wiggled her fingers, prosthetic metal digits moving with a fluidity no actual fingers could rival.

With all Blake had achieved, it was easy to forget she was completely human, but Eron saw it in this moment. Everything about Blake was leaden: the way she braced herself against the doorframe, the rigidity of her stance. Tension was holding her upright. Perhaps Kira saw it also, because she did not leave. And her voice was gentle when she next spoke.

'B, I'm sober enough, okay? Barely touched a drop.'

It might have been convincing if not for the vague slurring of the word 'drop'. Blake did not reply. She stepped deeper into the tech room, and the door closed.

Kira's shoulder's drooped. 'What is with her, E? She looks like hell.'

She turned, too quickly, and her inebriated state sent her wildly off balance. Eron's arms raised before he could halt himself. He embraced her. Their height differential saw her feet lifted off the ground. She tilted her head, and her breath was warm against the base of his throat. The scent of alcohol reached him.

'Ah, Eron. You always know how to make a girl feel better.' Kira laughed, a light mockery in her tone. Flippant with word and deed, she was as unsettling as she had ever been.

Eron needed to let go, move away from her right now. His hand drifted down her back, tracing the familiar curve. Her amber eyes made their soft way over his face. Ludicrous. How this diminutive creature could blur the world around him. A soul of Kur lay just a few paces away, yet he was caught here, barricaded from that miracle by this disorderly emotion.

Enough.

He let her go, but Kira moved faster than her current state should allow and wrapped her arms around his neck. She dangled there, feet off the ground, hanging against him like a strange human blanket.

'Kira –'

'Just one more second, okay? I know, I know, no touchy-feely, but indulge me. No one's here to see – the fun police are at prayer duty, right? I'm sorry you got ass-kicked over it all, I'm really sorry. I promise just this, then no more.'

Eron tilted forward, bending so that Kira's feet touched the ground. Her hands slipped down to wrap around his waist. Good judgement dictated that he push her away. He was the usual disappointment to himself. They stood pressed together, the top of her head soft against his mouth. The air was thick, and his senses chaotic with the touch of her.

'She's not doing so good, is she, E?' she mumbled against his chest. 'Is she okay?'

He breathed into the black strands of her hair. 'Your sister is strong.'

'Yeah, but she's human.'

She took a long, slow breath, and he felt the press of her breasts against him. Another opportunity to let go arrived and then slid away. But he promised himself, just this, then no more. As it should be. As it should have always been.

'See, just a few seconds. Like I promised.' Kira slid her arms free, brushing her fingertips across his waist. She gave him a lopsided smile, and then she was following after her sister as steadily as could be expected of her. The door opened, then closed again, removing her from his view. But Eron did not follow straight away. Taking a moment to find a decorum he would not lose again.

BLAKE - 6

Blake rushed to the back of the tech room, pulling a slender glass vial from a stainless steel drawer. Kira would follow. There was little doubt of that, so Blake had to make the most of the momentary solitude. Her shaking hands caused the vial to clatter against her teeth. Perhaps the tension of the morning had gotten to her. The sudden desire for the Waters had caught her off-guard. The liquid seared through her mouth, tracing a warm path down her throat. Blake tensed, bracing for the heat that would come with the movement of the Waters into her stomach and through her blood. The drive to suck back more was nearly insurmountable, but there could only be this – the barest portion – while Cym investigated more thoroughly, exactly what the Waters were doing to Blake's cells. Nothing good. That much was clear. So infuriatingly obvious. The weight loss and the unhealthy pallor of her skin might as well be a flashing neon sign – *Blake Beckworth is unwell.*

Sound the bells, ring the alarms, indeed. Kira was correct. She had made a mistake. Several, most likely, but the repercussions of this one were closest to home. She'd indulged Tamas's desire to convince her his boss truly was a supernatural being. A god. He'd wanted her to see what he saw, experience the events he believed he experienced. And in a moment of weakness, Blake had allowed herself to want to believe, too.

Several months ago, she'd sipped the Waters. The hallucinogenic trip was impressive, but so were those reported by users of DMT and LSD. The experiment hardly constituted a declaration of the existence of divinity. And the repercussions of the experiment were dire. Whatever immunity Tamas had to the effects of the alien liquid, Blake did not share them. So, now this. A gradual but irrefutable deterioration of her cells. A decline only slowed by a minimal but regular intake of the very Water that had impaired them to begin with. Cym, the only one who knew of the situation, was doing what he could to find a solution. In the interim, Blake was a dying addict.

She tossed the vial into a nearby trash can, making sure the evidence of her incapacity fell beneath the rest of the rubbish. Hidden. Her hands already steady. The irony didn't escape her. She'd lectured Kira for years about her addictions, the drink, the drugs, the sex. The media had been merciless about pointing out what a fuck-up Kira was compared to her, and how Blake's brains had funded Kira's veins – one of the cleverer headlines – for years. Yet, here Blake was. The furtive junkie, struggling not to think about the next time she could take a sip, one eye constantly on her watch. If Kira was in remotely anywhere near this much pain, then she was even stronger than Blake had accounted for. A good thing, considering what she was going to ask of her.

Blake shifted her newly arrived clarity to the control panel in front of her. From the moment Tamas had left, she'd been slowly dropping the inhibitor levels on the carapace. She glanced at the body. Azrael. Eron might have been unimpressed with the naming, but the Syranians could not dictate everything Blake did. She would have this, at least. Pride swelled, as it did every time she glanced at the perfectly formed humanoid. The machines surrounding him emitted cautioning beeps. A message flashed on the small screen, advising that containment dosage was low, asking if she wished to continue. She pressed in an affirmative.

The tech room door slid open and Kira stalked in.

'Surprise,' she declared. 'All your dreams have come true, I decided to stay. Holy shitballs! Blake made herself a boyfriend.' Clapping her hands, Kira danced up to the table where the carapace lay. 'That is the prettiest robot I've ever seen.'

'Move back, Kira. And stop talking bullshit.'

The girl had no capacity to take anything seriously. Pretty? No one called Michelangelo's David or the Artemision Bronze 'pretty'. They were works of art, superb in their perfection.

And, like Azrael, they were not robots.

For ease of access to his chest cavity, Blake had dressed Azrael only in a pair of pale-green linen pants, doctors' scrubs she'd taken from the medical ward up on ground level. Very little of his slender, muscular body was hidden. Each swell of muscle and curve of bone was exquisite. Every strand of his black hair, caught in a loose ponytail at the nape, had a manufactured medulla, cortex, and cuticle. Fine vellus hair covered his skin, just as it would have if he were a living, breathing man. His skin itself was a carefully constructed shade, olive with a rich golden undertone, as though the sun touched him, even down here in the bowels of the Earth.

Eron entered the room, bending forward through the doorway to accommodate his height. He stopped just inside the door, and his eyes fixed on Azrael, the muscles in his sharp jaw working.

'Is something wrong, Eron?' Blake asked, fingers hovering over the control panel. The inhibitor gases that turned the carapace from a functioning work of art to a solid, immovable lump of Telteriun had dropped to a level that the machine deemed unwise.

The Syranian did not answer her. He seemed incapable of doing so. Eron shook his head side to side slowly. She'd seen similar expressions on the faces of his colleagues last night. Shock and awe. She liked to think it was for her design prowess. It wasn't of course. She might be ill, but she was not stupid.

'What are these guys for?' Kira had not stepped away as she'd been instructed. And she poked her finger into Azrael's shoulder. 'Are they like sex toys or something? About time there was one for girls. Good for you, sis. This will bring in billions –'

'For god's sake, K. Grow up.' Blake scowled. Her sister's well-documented sexual appetite was voracious. Yet another trait they did not share.

An automated voice from the machine notified Blake of what she already saw: movement in Azrael's right foot.

Kira shrieked. 'Shit, it's a real dude? You could have warned me.' She wiped her hands against her jacket, finally stepping away from the bench.

'It is not a human. And I did not give you permission to touch it.' Cuffs held Azrael's wrists in place, retarding any violent movement of his arms, but she'd not locked the restraints at his ankles. Blake tapped in a command to halt the withdrawal of the inhibitors any further.

'He's warm and soft, Blake. I know you probably don't know it, but that's how humans feel. What kind of fucking shit are you doing down here, anyway? Human experimentation is so not cool.'

It had been long enough since she'd spent any reasonable time with Kira that she'd forgotten how much her sister's sarcasm affected her. Like nails on chalkboard. 'I've told you, it is not human.'

Kira snapped her flesh fingers. 'Pretty robot, nailed it the first time. And, I have to say, I would nail this. He is fine. B, you've outdone yourself. I totally get why you wanted to show this off. So cute, seeing you all proud and stuff. Don't you think, Eron?'

She beamed at smile at the alien, but Eron had eyes only for Azrael.

'Technician, the gallu appears to be active. Is that wise?' Eron drew in closer but, Blake noted, kept distance between himself and the prone carapace.

'He's contained. There's no need for concern.' Blake's stomach made an unpleasant gurgling sound, as though resoundingly disagreeing. 'And you are here. Added security, in the highly unlikely event we might need it.'

Spoken with confidence she didn't truly feel. She hadn't slept since the Meld, her mind churning over and over what she'd witnessed. A mind she was beginning to doubt. Blake's gaze darted to Azrael's fingertips. There was some movement beginning there as well. Sculpted, slender fingers. Genuine keratin made up the fingernails. But they would never grow. The humanness of Azrael was a mirage. But it was what lay at the core that she wanted so badly to see again. Wanted her sister to witness. Kira was the most human person Blake knew. And she called things completely as she saw them. If Blake doubted her own mind, she did not doubt Kira's.

Azrael's movements grew more pronounced.

'Step back, Kira,' Blake said. The alien metal, Telteriun, was dense, and the carapaces were easily half a tonne in weight. Eron was keeping too great a distance to shield her if anything untoward happened. Blake cursed her decision not to cuff Azrael's ankles. These kind of oversights were growing more pronounced.

Kira actually did as she was told and moved a few steps back, while Eron edged to the foot of the bench. Azrael's mouth opened. Then closed again, hard, with an audible crack of teeth. Blake frowned at the thought of what that pressure might do to the ceramic teeth installed in his jaw. His right leg jerked, bending slightly at the knee. His arms stiffened straight, and his fingers splayed, as though a mild seizure were making its way through his limbs. But his eyes did not open.

'Come on,' Blake breathed. 'Let us see you.'

Before last night, when Tamas had stepped into those dark waters out in the chamber, Blake had been certain of herself and her purpose. This was all just tech, incredibly advanced and stupefying perhaps, but artificial nonetheless. Ultimately understandable.

Azrael opened his eyes. A vibrant mix of green and rusty brown, just as she had made them. But they were still, fixed on one point. Not really seeing.

'And the boy has pretty eyes, too.' Kira's voice wavered. 'B, is your little friend supposed to be doing this?'

'Yes.'

He was. Just technically not yet. Not without the captain and the full contingent of Syranians present. Blake took Azrael's chin between her fingers, moving his head side to side, trying to get the eyes to focus. She did not realise that Kira had stepped up to the table until Eron cautioned her.

'I believe that is close enough, Kira. Please keep your distance,' he said.

'You keep yours,' Kira sniffed.

Azrael wrenched his left arm free of the restraint,

snapping the cuff as though it were made of candy, and grabbed Kira's jacket. She made a strangled sound as he wrenched her forward.

'Fuck me!' Kira cried, falling across Azrael's chest, face buried in his shoulder.

Eron dove forward, grabbing Kira's waist. 'Blake, immobilise the gallu!' he shouted.

But she didn't need any instruction. Blake raced back to the control panel, her hip catching the corner of the bench and the impact making her wince.

'Christ almighty, Blake. Do something.' Kira struggled against the arm pressing her down, managing to lift her head, which put her almost cheek to cheek with Azrael, who had, so far, thankfully not utilised his unbound legs. 'Let me go, robot. Lemme go. This is fucking rude –'

Kira fell silent. Blake's head jerked up, her heart thumping a mad beat against her chest. For a terrible second, she thought Kira had been silenced.

She had, but not in the way Blake feared.

Kira held up her metal hand to ward back Eron, whose face was creased with angry concern. Azrael still held her, but the embrace was no longer oppressive, allowing Kira to edge back enough so that she leaned over him, her face just above his. A sound came from Azrael's mouth. A strangled push of air that might have been a groan. His gaze zigzagged through the air around Kira's face. Beginning to focus. Blake's fingers rested on the control panel. One press and she would render the carapace immovable. But she hesitated.

'Hey, buddy. Wanna let me go?' Kira's voice dipped low in the silent room. Gentle. Intimate. Blake glanced at the keys beneath her fingers, oddly uncomfortable.

A louder, more urgent groan escaped Azrael, and in an instant the quiet moment was shattered. He jerked his body, hips lifting and the waistband of his pants slipping down low over his pelvis. He pushed Kira away, and his strength saw her catapult across the room. She let the world know what she thought of Blake's creation as she went, crashing into the far wall.

'Kira!' Blake cried.

But Azrael wasn't done. He swung his legs off the table, throwing his full body weight against the last remaining cuff. It might as well have been made of tinfoil.

In just a few seconds chaos had taken over the room.

'The inhibitors!' Eron threw himself against Azrael, forcing him back down to the table.

'Kira?' Blake couldn't see her sister over the struggling pair, but there was no answer. Her body shook, her legs barely able to hold her as her fingers flew over the keypad. Christ, what had she done? Familiar warning signals blasted her. Inhibitor levels were too high, but she wanted them higher. They needed to be higher. She looked up. Eron had Azrael face down against the stainless-steel tabletop, bending Azrael's free arm up behind his back like a highway cop making an arrest. Azrael lifted his head, strands of his dark hair across his face.

Forest-green eyes met hers. Actually zeroed in on her, with no hint of the blinded panic of earlier. Blake's breath caught in her throat. She scanned his eyes, searching for a hint of what lay inside the carapace. Azrael stared at her until the inhibitors made it impossible. His body slumped against the table. Eron waited a few seconds before releasing him. The Syranian's topknot had come loose in the fray, rendering his silver-white hair uncharacteristically messy around his face. His breathing quickened by the effort it took to restrain Azrael.

The electronic beeps from the machine made Blake's ears ring. Her fingers shook even harder than they had earlier, and her feet refused to allow her to move to where she could see her sister. She squeezed her eyes shut, trying to force back the images that flickered. The blood, the grey hue of Kira's face as they'd rushed her into the medical ward. The flashbacks had gotten so much worse since the Waters. At times she heard her father's voice. So clear she expected to see him standing over her. Hallucinations. Nothing more. But they were growing so strong that she'd found herself answering questions no one had asked her. Called out to people who were not there.

'Holy crapping Jesus, Blake. What was that?'

Blake's eyes flew open. Eron was helping Kira to her feet.

'Are you all right, Kira?' he said.

'Yeah, I'm good.'

But the Syranian seemed unconvinced. He brushed back her hair, and his hand cupped her cheek. A hint of their intimacy evident in the way he pressed his body towards her, placing a barrier between her and things that might harm her. Blake looked away. *Had* harmed her. If ever there was a reason to suspect one's own mental instability, then surely the moment Blake had made the decision to bring Kira down here, was it.

Blake turned her gaze to Azrael. Now still. Lying as Eron had left him, on his side on the table. The two marks between Azrael's shoulder blades, ten-centimetre incisions that radiated at diagonal angles from his spine, were further evidence that Blake's state of mind was not as it should be. What lay beneath the marks were fanciful additions, showpieces that served no real purpose except to give Blake opportunity to act like some overindulged toy-maker.

'Blake?' Kira stood right beside her now, and the proximity, as it always did, sent flutters of unease through

Blake. 'Stop shitting me. This dude is human, isn't he? B, look at me.'

But Blake didn't wish to. Not because of what she'd see on Kira's face, but because of what her sister might see on hers.

'He was so fucking scared, Blake. I mean, did you see his eyes? Shit-scared. If he's not human, then why would you program a robot to act so damn freaked out?'

She hadn't. It was that level of code enhancement Blake expected to be working on after Tamas and the Syranians were done at the First Meld. She'd believed it would take weeks of work to get the reactions and reaction times right. Enable Azrael to act human. Blake folded her arms and pushed unsteady hands against a far-too-prenounced ribcage, considering her answer.

Eron had not followed Kira. He stood alone on the opposite side of the room. 'Kira, what you have witnessed here is not –'

'Fear is a human emotion,' Blake interjected. 'A powerful one, and he needs to pass for human.'

There was actually a layer of truth to the lie. As per Tamas's instructions, the carapaces had to be convincingly human. They had to breathe at rates matching physical output, cry real tears, blush, shiver. Tremble.

'You're telling me he's just a robot?' Kira demanded.

Eron shifted but stayed silent, and Blake finally looked at her sister. She held Kira's gaze.

'Yes. It's just a robot.'

TAMAS - 7

Tamas had sat in on each daily training session for a week now, watching the Syranians hone their command of the mea stones. Nari ensured he had an adequate seat each time, but his discomfort had deepened into something beyond physical. Tamas uncrossed his legs, shaking a foot that tingled with pins and needles.

'Do you wish to leave, sir?' Nari stood nearby, arms behind her back, shoulders locked back.

He shook his head. 'No, not yet.'

The guard nodded, opening her mouth to speak, just as another agonised screech erupted from the pit at the centre of the room. Tamas jumped, and gritted his teeth at his inability to act nonplussed. It was hardly the first time he'd heard Azrael cry out in pain, but today's session appeared particularly brutal. Captain Nex pushed his god-soldiers with a fervour Tamas didn't recognise from the past few days. Everyone was getting restless, impatient to move on. So far as Nex was concerned, the Syranians had mastered control of their mea stones. Each day he watched Tamas more intently, searching for any sign that Ereshkigal deemed them ready to handle what would come next. *Who* would come next. The Four, the most formidable of all the gallu in her realm.

Tamas approached the railing that ran the perimeter of the training area, a wide space several feet below: one entranceway in, one entranceway out. An unfinished elevator shaft originally, accessed via level ten, widened and deepened to accommodate Captain Nex's requirements. Apparently, he required something akin to an ancient Roman fighting pit. Leaning over the rail, Tamas fixed his eyes on the group below. Azrael kneeling, surrounded by the Syranians. So much beauty amidst such cruelty. Not just Blake's ridiculously sculpture-perfect design for Azrael, but the Syranians themselves, moving with the grace of deadly dancers. Their curious mix of muscle and refinement, solid frames encasing delicate features, was certainly mesmerising, alluring he supposed, when he had the strength and freedom to think about it.

'Parator, again.' Captain Nex strode around the space like a flippant matador. 'You hesitate too long. Strike hard. Always. You are master.'

The Syranian soldier, the youngest in the group, saluted his leader, curling his hand into a fist and pressing the side of his upturned palm against his chest. The mark of respect always reminded Tamas of someone driving a dagger into their own heart.

'Yes, Captain.' Parator's voice echoed off the concrete walls. 'The gallu is tiring, I believe.'

The aliens' voices were as wistful as their features, their native tongue a weird mix of the roughness of a language like Russian and a softer twang like Danish. Difficult to get a human tongue around, but with Cym and Gren's assistance, Tamas had managed. One benefit to the aliens' lack of irises – stark-white eyeballs with a bare smudge of colour beneath – was that Tamas could imagine himself speaking to blind people. If he deluded himself into thinking he was not being scrutinised visually, the anxiety stayed buried.

'It is you who are tiring, Parator. And if you commanded one of the Four right now, and not this pathetic creature, then you would have already lost control. You would have failed your Lord Lahar. Now, you will continue until there is no strength remaining, in either you or the gallu.' Nex's ever-present annoyance deepened his pitch. 'Continue until that mea stone burns your very flesh.'

Parator glanced down at the sand-coloured stone

embedded in his forearm, as if he expected to see the skin already glowing with embers. His eyes lifted towards Bel and Gren, but his fellow soldiers offered only cool, detached stares.

'Seder!' the captain roared. 'Commence attack.'

Seder raised a weapon, a sword for all intents and purposes, with three peaks running the length of the blade. His movement shifted his gleaming silver hair, gathered in a ponytail against his back, its tip sweeping against the base of his spine. Of all the aliens, Seder was the least likeable. Vain and sullen. Treating his precious hair better than he ever did Tamas.

Seder thrust the weapon at Azrael, and the gallu's natural instinct to defend itself was, yet again, used against it. Azrael pushed to his feet, letting loose with another of his strangled, animalistic cries, and launched at Seder. The god-soldier pirouetted out of reach, and Parator stepped forward. Directly into the path of the raging, flailing gallu.

The hollow-cheeked Syranian didn't so much as flinch as a tonne of Telteriun metal hurtled at him. He lifted his left arm every so slightly, and Azrael jerked as though he'd hit a wall. Tamas cringed at the ear-shattering sound that flew from the embattled gallu. He quickly cleared his expression. If any of the Syranians happened to glance up, they must see a Messenger who was steady, focused. One who was taking in every inch of the scene so that the goddess had a front-row seat when he took his memories to the shrine for her viewing.

Parator took a step towards Azrael, who was clawing at the air in front of him as though trying to shred the molecules themselves. The gallu did not shift from his position. He could not. Parator used the stone adeptly, exercising utter control over the hapless Azrael. Blake had been incessant with her questions about the workings of the ancient stones, but had been unhappy with Tamas's explanation. Surgically embedded into each Syranian before they had left their homeworld, the mea stones enhanced telepathic and telekinetic ability. They were relics, like the Tier Waters, from a distant past when the Syranian universe contained multiple gods. With further pieces worked into the structure of each carapace as Blake had constructed them, the pieces of stone – innocuous as rubble – became powerful remote-control units, enabling the Syranians to exercise utter control over the metal, and in turn, the beings within.

Seder danced forward and sliced the sword across the gallu's bare chest. This time there was impact, the tip of the blade making a great slice in the faux flesh. Tamas shuddered. Despite knowing that the skin was artificial, and the flowing blood man-made, the sight was no less disconcerting. Added to that was the knowledge that Azrael was being stripped of his ability to defend himself. Parator, through sheer, brutal will, forced the gallu's arms wide, dragged him to his knees, and arched his back at an angle that looked fit to crack any calcium-based spine.

Parator was bullying Azrael into submission, overpowering a creature whose natural strength was ten times Parator's own. Treating him little better than a rag doll he'd grown tired of. Tamas crossed his arms, stifling his empathy for the enraged creature and digging his fingernails through the thin fabric of his faded blue shirt.

'I've seen enough today.' Tamas strode past Nari, who fell into line alongside. They made quick progress out of the training area. He could not close the door fast enough on the scene behind him. Once in the elevator, Nari paused with her hand over the buttons.

'Where to, sir?'

Tamas took a deep breath, finally loosening his fingers and letting his arms fall to his sides. 'Orientation Room. I'll do the memory transfer now.' *Get it over with*, he stopped himself from saying.

'Very well,' Nari said, entering the code for the floor. 'I'll remain with you.'

It wasn't a question; and Tamas had no intention of protesting. He raised his hand to his mouth, covering his smile with a cough.

'Are you unwell?' Nari's face gave nothing away, dark eyes steely, mouth set in a hard line, as if she were daring him to be anything but perfect. But at least she'd asked.

'I'm fine.'

That would change in about half an hour. The transfer at the shrine made him bone tired; five days straight of it would be a record. One he wasn't keen to set, but the goddess had better things to do than be present at day after day of Syranian training. The goddess had attended the very first of these training sessions, but for the past week had been occupied with her own affairs. She was in the midst of a divine war, after all. What was going on here, on Earth, was a footnote in her battle plans. Tamas understood that. The goddess was in his head, and all her irritation and impatience and distraction with it. As self-important as Captain Nex believed himself and his little god Lahar to be, truth was his whole mission was the proverbial Hail Mary. A long shot in an epic, long-running battle taking place worlds away.

Ereshkigal was playing every card available to her, however unlikely to succeed. She commanded them to find a single soul, that of Dumuzi— a demigod condemned thousands of years ago to an eternal cycle of life and death on Earth—and replace his soul with another, far more dangerous one. Ereshkigal's most nefarious enemy. Her very own sister, the goddess of war – Inanna. This was a vicious, deeply personal war that raged, and from what Tamas had witnessed of the relationship between mortal sisters Blake and the annoying little bitch she called a sibling, he could barely imagine the scale of the calamity that existed between the goddesses. Hatred and unfathomable love seemed to run in twin streams, both equally as deep. And dark.

'Sir?'

Nari gestured to the opened elevator door. Tamas jerked upright, forgetting he was not alone.

'Yes, yes.' He hurried past her, ignoring the twinge in his back muscles, an ache that had increased with the activities of the past week. 'I won't be long.'

They moved into the expanse of the domed Orientation Room, and Tamas strode into the shrine, trying to add a swagger to his movement that suggested he wasn't dreading the discomfort to follow. His toe caught on the top step, and he stumbled forward. Cursing beneath his breath, Tamas knelt at the base of the petrified tree trunk at the centre of the shrine, a copper bowl atop the wide girth of the long-dead tree containing a portion of the Tier Waters. More of the liquid flowed between the glass panels making up the walls and ceiling, setting the world around him afire with emerald light. He bowed his head, fighting the urge to scratch at the base of his chin. Clipping his beard was well overdue. Perhaps, after he slept, he'd attend to it.

He whispered the utterances taught, or rather drummed, into him by his mother. Sacred words and devotions passed down through generations, originating with the very first of Tamas's line, the Abgal Utuabzu. One of seven sages created by the great Enki, the god of knowledge, and sent to mankind to instruct them on creating civilisation. The Abgal were demigods, immensely powerful beings. Utuabzu's blood ran in Tamas's veins – however diluted it may be after thousands of years of the gods' absence – yet he could barely manage to pronounce the sage's name without stuttering. That would be over soon. A job well done would be rewarded by the goddess. His mother had told him that Ereshkigal would reignite the divine blood coursing through them if they served her well. The Abgal's power would be rebirthed.

Tamas stood up and lowered his hands into the Tier Waters. The sooner he could shed this pathetic human carcass the better. A holy sage would not tremble in front of strangers, they wouldn't stumble up the stairs of the shrine. The fluid seeped beneath his nails and into his pores, achingly cold. He raised his eyes and met the glare of Ereshkigal's totem, the Arabian wolf, carved into the roof above him. One crystal eye flickered. A palm-sized paw bulged from the glass. So often he flinched when the wolf launched itself from the glass, transforming from two-dimensional to three. More times than he cared to count, Tamas would tremble, hunch in fear as the enormous jaws widened and clamped down on his skull, beginning their feast on his memories. But each time he managed to maintain eye contact with the approaching manifestation just a little longer.

The fangs pierced the soft flesh at his temples, and he bit down hard on his lip to stem his cry. Not a sound today, though tears pricked at his eyes. He lowered his lids, and the memories of Azrael's training flashed through his head, a video recording on high speed transferring into the glass wolf, and in turn flowing through to the goddess. His hands shook so violently the Waters sloshed against the floor. But still he didn't utter a sound.

Even if the pressure burst all the blood vessels in his eyes, he would hold his ground. Show everyone, everyone that counted, that he was worthy of the demigod ghosting within his DNA.

Buried in concentration, Tamas staggered at the sudden release of the wolf's jaws. The flow of memories vanished, and blackness filled his mind. He blinked but the darkness didn't shift. He tried to lift his hands from the Waters, but it was as though the liquid had frozen around his wrists, locking him in place. A curl of panic unfurled before sound exploded in his skull, like a chorus of insane angels screeching at him through a megaphone. Tamas's knees buckled, and his stomach heaved. His lips parted, and he might have been screaming but it was impossible to tell.

Silence chased back the chaos, leaving Tamas alone with the ringing in his ears. But he smiled. Laughter lifted from him, high and mildly maniacal.

Finally, the goddess had bestowed on him the gift she'd afforded his mother.

Prescience.

This world was a footnote no longer. In two short days, they would rise. The Four would walk the Earth. He had seen it. Tears streamed down Tamas's face, and his lips ached with the width of his smile.

'Tamas?' Nari called to him from beyond the shrine. A small and distant voice. 'Tamas, is everything all right?'

Straightening, Tamas rose from his knees and called out, sure and steady. 'Everything is fine.'

KIRA - 8

Kira jabbed her fingertip into the impressive bubblegum balloon. It popped against her chin, and with an absent-minded stroke, she twirled the sticky mess around her finger.

'I'm totally authorised to be here, Weylen. Chill.' She offered the nervous biotech a smile, hoping it looked mildly genuine. 'Check if you want, but we all know Super Sis is busy as hell and doesn't tolerate questions well when she's swamped. Am I right?'

Kira hoped like fuck she was. Truthfully, she had no clue what type of boss her sister was. But considering that she sucked as a sister, Kira was going with the impatient-bitch model. And the busy part was true enough. In the past couple of days, the vibe had changed down here in the guts of the place. Everyone seemed so god-damn busy, couldn't lift their eyes from their tablets and charts to say boo when she walked past. Blake hadn't said more than good morning in the past week since that weird four-in-the-morning call. *Come see what I made, Kira. Now piss off and forget about it.*

What the hell was that all about?

'Kira, we really don't have time for –' Gwen Weylen hesitated, tugging at one of the crazy curly strands of black hair framing her face. Blake's right-hand chick. Probably knew her better than Kira did, but Gwen's flustered demeanour said she knew about Kira, too.

'Time for my shit?' Kira crossed her legs and leaned against the glass of Azrael's containment cell, gesturing to the half-naked guy lying on the concrete floor staring at them. 'All I'm doing is chatting. Shooting the breeze. He doesn't seem to mind my shit. Finds it more interesting than trying to crack open his pretty skull on the rock. Which is what he was doing when I arrived. Did you see that?'

Slight exaggeration. He had been curled up in a ball in a corner, rocking back and forth, his bare back thudding against the rock.

Gwen tightened her arms around her chest, pushing ample breasts even higher beneath her lab coat. No doubt about it, the girl kept some impressive secrets under that god-awful coat. 'We did . . . I did observe that, yes. He returns from training displaying heightened levels of trauma.' Her gaze grew distant, resting on Azrael. He lay on his side, in the middle of the empty space, dark hair loosened from its tie, strands falling across his cheek. Shirtless for some unknown reason, hair mussed up as if he'd just banged a football team. If the dude hadn't looked so freaked out, if the cell hadn't looked so much like a damn cell, then it would have made an awesome model shoot. The lighting was right. All globes blazing. The compartment lit up like a fucking Christmas tree. Turns out pretty boy had issues. The dude went supernova nuts if he was left in the dark.

'Yeah well, whatever Captain Asshat's *training* involves,' Kira said, 'Az here doesn't like it. Not one little bit.' Speaking of asshats, Eron had disappeared from Blake's powwow a week ago and was avoiding Kira like the proverbial plague. She swore the guy had a tracking device on her so he could make sure he was always somewhere else. 'You know what, you guys should be thanking me, I'm looking after the merchandise. Look at him. I'm either so boring, or so mesmerising, that he forgets his android troubles when I'm around.' She winked at Gwen. 'I think we both know which of those two it is.'

The biotech had obviously been born without a funny bone. 'Kira, I have about fifteen minutes of work to do in the tech room. You will leave with me when I'm done. Do you understand? And this will be the last time you come down here.'

'Yes, Mum.'

'I'm serious. I let yesterday slide, but it wasn't an open invitation to wander around the high-security areas everyday.'

'I said yes, Mum. What more do you want from me?'

'For you to listen.'

'Listening.'

'Good. Fifteen minutes.' Gwen pulled a tablet from the copious pockets of her coat and walked away, jabbing in whatever biotechs jabbed into those things.

Fucking hell. Things were definitely off down here. Yesterday morning, Kira had thought for certain Gwen would chase her out when she'd wandered down in the early hours. But nope. So Kira'd pushed it again, returning the same time today, right about the time the aliens had their prayer session to Lah-Lah or whatever their supreme leader's name was.

Kira returned her attention to robo-boy. 'Everyone's so distracted. What the hell's going on, Az? And why does no one seem to want to play with you anymore, did you chuck too many tanties?'

No answer, of course not. If the dude worked out how to use those sleek lips of his, she'd have a fucking heart attack. Even yesterday when she'd seen him banging his back against the wall, he hadn't made a sound.

Blake had never explained why they needed glass cells built

on level eleven. Now Kira knew. Apparently they were some kind of shitty android Holiday Inn. The spaces were barely big enough to contain a single bed, which was good considering no one had bothered to put any furniture in anyway. And Az clearly didn't need to shit and piss, because there was no sign of a toilet, or even a sink for water. The cells ran along the back of the cavern, the bare rock forming the rear walls.

'Okay, where was I?' she said. 'Right, explaining the movie. So the twist. Get this, he was totally kissing his sister. And the audience knows it. Gross, right?' She tapped her metal fingers against the glass panel that separated her from the prone body of pretty robo-boy. 'Still with me, Az? It's a classic movie. If Tamas and Blake weren't such Neanderthals, they'd give you a PlayStation or something down here. Let you watch some stuff, play a few games. Not sure how you'd go with games, though. You're not exactly the sharpest tack in the box, huh?'

Az just stared, unblinking. Emerald eyes like two perfect circles of jade. Fucking gorgeous. And the wild-eyed look she'd seen in the tech room was gone; now it was more like a newborn kid's. Not quite focusing but getting damn close, eyelids widening and lowering, as though he didn't quite understand how he was making them move at all. Maybe they still had him dosed to the brim with that sedative thing Blake and Eron had shouted about when he'd first gone ballistic.

'What's going on down here? Are they like prepping the ship or something?' Kira mused to the unresponsive Azrael. 'Like, maybe the aliens are leaving 'cause you're all done. Is that it? Mission accomplished?'

She blinked away the vision of Eron that flickered in her head.

'Fuck him.' Kira glanced at her watch. She hadn't been awake and sober at six thirty in the morning since they'd checked her out of intensive care three years ago. Her gaze wandered over Azrael's bare torso. The boy had some impressive dips and rises. 'What's with that? I mean, seriously, no complaints, but I'm pretty sure the budget can cover a T-shirt.'

Being forced to look at a chest that had curves like the fucking Sahara shouldn't bug her this much. She liked half-naked men almost as much as fully naked men, but something about it — how exposed it seemed to make him, like a giant featherless baby bird — pissed her off. In fact, a lot about him pissed her off, and she had no clue why. Hadn't gotten the bastard out of her head since the morning he'd cracked one of her ribs. The fear had something to do with it, the all-too-clear shadow of horror in his eyes when Blake had brought him to life. Programming, Blake said. Cruelty to fucking androids, Kira said. What asshole would purposely enable something to be that scared?

She knew that fear.

Kira ran the tip of her flesh fingers over the glass, tracing the outline of Azrael's body. 'I hope you appreciate this, mate. I could be at my pub, watching Perry clean up vomit and spilled beer. Instead I'm sitting here babysitting your sorry ass 'cause you remind me of some sad bitch I know.'

She pointed a metal digit to the centre of her chest, right at the tip of the scar that ran most of the length of her sternum. The assumption might be that when aliens from an advanced world were involved in your surgery you might not end up stuck with a scar the size of Texas. Wrong. No memory wipes either, which would have been nice.

She couldn't hide from the memories of waking up in the medical ward, half her bloody parts missing, and a giant hole, the size of her dad, wrenched open in her life. Panic attacks were par for the course in the beginning. Fuck, those were the days. The sweet, sweet memories of sweating buckets in freakouts so violent she sometimes thought she might burst an eyeball. And more than once, after dousing her face with cold water, she'd stared into the bathroom mirror and seen the fear shadows. Her eyes just like Az's, vacant and intent all at once, wide as hell, as if there wasn't enough light in the world to chase back the darkness that wanted to swallow her up and eat her whole.

It was a blast.

'What's in your shadows, robo-boy?' Kira's breath whitened the glass. 'What tree did you drive into?'

She leaned her forehead against the glass, shooting out quick little breaths. It had been a long while since she'd had a full-on panic attack, and she didn't intend to start again now. Time to go back to the surface where the Earth didn't feel as though it were preparing to pummel her. A mimosa perhaps, to put a little brightness in her day. Kira uncrossed her legs, jigging them against the concrete, trying to work back some life into the limbs. Her butt ached.

'Blakey Blake, what are you up to down here?' Kira rocked onto her knees, and Azrael made a tiny movement. His first in about an hour. Hugged his hands in against his chest. 'Hey, it's okay. I'm not going to touch you. Not going to hurt you.'

There was that, too. If she moved a bit too quick, he acted as if she were about to beat his head in. She pushed to her feet, slow enough that her knees sent out 'cease and desist' jabs of pain. Az's gaze didn't leave her, and his hands slipped back onto the concrete, unclenched. Fuck she was tired. Time to sleep most of the day away. Probably should eat at some point too. Then maybe in the afternoon consider if this was the day she'd leave the Facility and go back out into the real world.

Where there were no shirtless robots with haunted faces, and abs to go to war over.

****

True to form, sleep took up a good chunk of the day. No thanks to the little pink pills she downed when she got back to her townhouse just after seven. By the time she resurfaced late in the afternoon, the niggling hunger pains had become a raging fire-storm of starvation.

Kira's stomach made a sound like a wookie giving birth. Pizza. Extra jalapeños. Kira could feel them now, jumping around in her stomach acid as if they were having a pool party. The chef had gone fucking nuts with this one, apparently so excited someone had ordered food that he'd thrown every damn ingredient at the base. Poor bloke must have been bored to tears cooking for Blake and Tamas mostly with Kira so rarely in her Facility townhouse. Those two sparrows seemed to live on air alone. Blake sure as hell looked like she did. How that half-mute asshat Tamas ran this place, Kira had no idea. The guy always looked as if he were going to puke a lung when she spoke to him, which was so rarely she couldn't remember when they'd last come face-to-face. She took a sip of freshly opened champagne.

A message blinked at her from her cell phone. Perry called hours ago, wanting to know if she was going to drag her ass into work and help him out at the Wheel and Barrow tonight.

It was six in the evening and she still hadn't decided on an answer. In the handful of times they'd spoken over the past week, Perry hadn't said a word about her going MIA, but there had been a note of wistfulness in his last message. And saying he needed help on a Tuesday, one of the quietest nights of the week, was his roundabout way of saying, *What the hell is going on?*

Really, she should go. Gwen made it abundantly clear she wouldn't be welcome back on level eleven anytime soon. And Blake was back to ignoring her. Kira had left her three messages. In hindsight, she probably shouldn't have left the last one while she was on the toilet. Niagra Falls in the background probably wasn't pleasant.

Kira waved her flesh hand towards the TV sensor, and it responded by bringing up the holographic control in front of her. She flicked through a dozen stations. If she were interested in the world's worst jobs or how to doomsday prep, she would be fine. Another flick and she caught a glimpse of a very familiar face. Her own. Leaving a nightclub in France somewhere. Messily. A rerun of some overpunctuated entertainment program.

'Yay me,' she declared to the sad, weeping fern that was the only other living thing in the apartment. 'Cannes was awesome, I'm told.'

She took another bubbly sip and tried Blake's number again, not entirely certain what it was she wanted to say to her sister. She decided she would start with hello. Or maybe not – straight to voicemail. Righto. Looked as though Blake's desire to actually talk to her sister had well and truly evaporated. Again. Kira should go. Book a one-way ticket somewhere. It had been Bali last time. Scotland was next on the list. Find out what's under the kilts.

'Leave the crazy bitch with her tin soldiers and ETs, and go get me a life.' Forget the android on the floor. And the silver-haired alien with the sweetest orgasm face she'd ever seen. 'Shit, where did that come from? Right, definitely time to get the hell out of here. I think I've got cabin fever.' She tugged at one of the fern fronds, and it came free of its stem.

'No wonder you're not saying much.' Kira flicked the dying green tendril onto the floor.

Her apartment door opened, and three people filed into the room. The first wore a grey jacket with the hood drawn up and face hidden, but behind them was the unmistakable bulk of Rossiter.

Then, shock of all fucking shocks, Blake followed in close behind him. Heading straight to the grey-hoodie person, guiding them to sit on the couch. Which they did, the way a hundred-year-old grandad might do it. Slow and not very steady.

'Okay.' Kira stood up, crossing her arms over her chest. She wore her favourite T-shirt, She-Ra Princess of Power faded across its front, and so threadbare her nipples threatened to poke heads to freedom. Safe bet her sister didn't want to see that. 'Blake, I gotta draw the line at an orgy with my own sister.'

Blake pushed the hood free from the mystery man's head and Kira's mouth dropped. Azrael. With a shirt on. And his hair bunched into a ponytail, one loose strand cupping the curve of his cheek. Looking like Kira often did. Half-baked.

'Hey, cupcake,' Kira said. 'Long time no see.'

Azrael's stare-fest moved to her lips as it often did, as if he couldn't work out why they were moving. But he wasn't alone in the staring competition today. Blake locked on to her like a hawk targeting a mouse.

'Your robot is in my lounge room.' Kira gestured to Azrael. 'Something you want to tell me, Blake?'

Hawkeye Beckworth shook her head. 'There's something I want you to do.'

BLAKE - 9

Blake crouched beside Azrael, and Rossiter loomed over them both. The overprotective bodyguard had failed to heed her repeated requests to leave. She'd said it politely enough to begin with, but her patience was running thin. She was acutely aware that there was only so long before someone realised she was looping the surveillance footage of Azrael's cell.

'Rossiter, I want you to leave –'

'I don't think this is a good idea, leaving you two alone with –' Rossiter's hand fluttered uselessly as he sought the word.

Blake considered standing, but just the thought of the energy that would take kept her on her knees.

'You are not required to think about my requests,' she said.

Harsh, without doubt, but since the death of their father – and Rossiter's former military colleague – the massively structured man had taken his job to a new level of commitment, acting as though Blake required not only security but guidance as well. An incorrect, and mildly irritating, assumption. She neither needed nor desired an alternate father figure. She'd make her own mistakes and clean them up without assistance.

'You can go now,' Blake said.

Muscles in Rossiter's thick neck danced with the indecision tightening his body. 'I'll wait on your call to return Azrael to level eleven.'

His gaze darted to Kira. The look on her face was discernible enough. Confusion. And Kira did not like to be confused. Blake had best get to the point, or her sister's irritation would make conversation laborious; sarcasm, innuendo, and crass language were always Kira's go-to when she became uncomfortable.

The door closed behind Rossiter with a gentle click. Kira stood behind the black leather couch, tapping her fingernails against her prosthetic, creating a dull sound. Despite the work Blake had put in to creating a perfect faux skin for the arm, Kira refused to wear it, and Blake's inability to view the bare prosthetic without feeling ill had not reduced over the years. She focused back on Azrael. The apartment smelled of pizza. A deep, rich scent that turned Blake's empty stomach. Two empty beer bottles, and an open champagne bottle sat beside the pizza box.

'I've just got to put it out there, B,' Kira said. 'I'm not sure I'm into the robot sex thing. I mean he's cute and everything, but this just isn't oiling my engine.'

She waved her hands over Azrael, who sat oblivious, maintaining his trance-like observance of the television. All at once doubt edged its way into Blake's mind. Earlier today she'd been so certain of what should occur. Gwen had informed her of Kira's visits to the containment cell. They'd both observed Azrael's favourable reaction to her presence, and had ensured it was not a one-off by allowing Kira to sit with him a second time this morning. For reasons Blake struggled to comprehend, the gallu appeared to find Kira's juvenile, trivial chatter soothing.

Blake shifted her shoulders, shrugging off her own discontent at allowing the term into her vocabulary. *Gallu.* A mythological Sumerian entity. A demon or devil. It both stupefied and intrigued her that the Syranians used a term derived from an ancient Earth religion, but it was hardly evidence that the energy contained in the carapace was anything remotely divine. Evidence of a superior intellectual race once having been on Earth? Perhaps. And if the Syranians were prepared to simply destroy that evidence, then what harm in keeping it for herself and attempting to understand both the gallu and the mea stone welded into the carapace. Captain Nex declared both disposable. Of the five carapaces, Azrael was the one she was most proud of. The Syranians treated him as little more than a crash-test dummy, a model that would be discontinued the moment the Four arrived to fill the empty shells awaiting them.

Taking a deep breath, Blake quietened the nagging doubt. Her hands were steady today, her thoughts clear. A suppressant Cym had given her the day before appeared to be blocking the hallucinatory and physical effects of the Waters. No mental impairment hindered her thought process today. No ache behind her eyes. Her usefulness to the Syranians was drawing to a close; she understood that. But it did not mean she had to go quietly. And she was fast running out of days. What little control she still held was about to be removed.

Blake forced herself to her feet. Despite the success of Cym's latest concoction, her limbs were leaden.

'Take him out,' she said.

Kira's eyes widened, and a choked laugh escaped her. 'Whoa. Okay. Well my gun's in the shop right now —'

'Don't be stupid, Kira. Listen to me. Take him out of

the Facility. Like you did with Eron.'

Now Kira's laughter was not choked. It was loud and free and full of incredulity. 'Oh, just like that? The thing that ended with him being banished to his room for months, and to this day makes the captain and Tamas look at me like I'm shit they just stepped in? Sure. No worries.'

'I don't have time —'

Kira's laughter evaporated. 'For my shit? No one fucking does. Especially you —'

'This is not the time.' Heat flushed Blake's face.

'Nah. Never is. Hasn't been for years.' Kira poured herself another golden, bubbling champagne. 'Just say it. You'll feel better.'

Blake frowned. 'What?'

Kira threw back the champagne before the froth had a chance to settle. 'Say it. You hate me. Hated me since the day I slammed Dad into a tree.' A crack infiltrated her tone.

Now it was Blake's turn for incredulity. Of all the moments for this mammoth conversation to burst free of the carefully packed box both she and Kira had shoved it into, this was truly the most inopportune. 'Kira . . . I don't . . .' Reality was too complex for a hurried discussion. And the death of their father had created a rich tapestry, as difficult to look at as Kira's arm. Did she blame Kira for the accident? Blake had not stopped long enough to allow herself to give it consideration. But hate her sister? No. Blake loathed herself. For not pulling Kira out of the pit she'd descended into since that day. While Kira drowned, Blake submerged herself, and her grief, in the alien world, with all the advanced technology and artificial life she could gorge on.

'Kira, listen to me.' Blake grabbed the bottle before Kira could pour another glass. 'I need you to focus. On this. Right now. This moment. The past will have to wait.'

'What's another three years, right?'

The waft of Kira's alcohol-and-garlic-scented breath pushed Blake back a step. 'You went out in public more than once with an extraterrestrial. Somehow you managed to integrate Eron into everyday situations –'

'Trust me, the Ballers Club is so far from an everyday –'

'My point, Kira, if you will allow me to make it, is that you have a talent for manipulation –'

'You're just laying on the fucking compliments, aren't you? Give me the bottle.'

'No.' Blake scanned the room. The layout was identical to her own townhouse one block down. She strode into the kitchen and tipped the near-full bottle over the sink.

'Jesus, that's a four-hundred-dollar bottle,' Kira cried. 'Are you fucking kidding me?'

She reached for the bottle, her hands getting in the way of the fleeing liquid, sending sugar-brown specks over Blake's white linen blouse. The simmering anger rose up again, and before Blake realised what she'd done, she slammed an open palm against Kira's flesh shoulder, sending her sister stumbling against the sink.

'What the fuck was that for, you crazy bitch?' Kira rubbed at the small of her back. 'Christ almighty, go back to ignoring me. I'm good with that.'

They stood close in the narrow kitchen. Reason suggested now may be a good time to reach for Kira, tend to her, ensure she was not injured. Blake folded her arms across her unstable stomach and moved away.

'Kira, I've not behaved in the way I should have. Not just now, and perhaps not in the past. For that, I apologise. But any further discussion must wait. This is too important. I need one thing from you. Take Azrael out of here. You have to make him blend in, the same way you managed with Eron. He must be made invisible.' She paused, and decided on frankness. 'I believe you may be the only one who can.'

'You mean I'm the freak with special clearance at the gate.' Kira brandished her metal prosthetic, waving her fingers in Blake's face. She was not incorrect. Blake had taken into account that the extraterrestrial properties of Kira's limb meant the Lucentshield surrounding the Facility required momentary shut-off at any entranceway Kira used, allowing her entry and exit without setting off alarms. A force field for all intents and purposes, the Lucentshield was originally designed to conceal the energy readings emanating from the Waters.

Frowning, Blake pushed her sister's hand away. 'That is part of it, yes. But you also understand human behaviour —'

'In a way that you don't.'

Blake ground her teeth, refusing to be baited. There wasn't time for an argument. If she was to secure Kira's assistance in removing Azrael from the Facility, the personal slights her sister was so fond of must be allowed to slide. Blake removed a device from her pocket: a wristband, finger-width wide, with several coloured panels on its matte silver surface. 'Azrael is mildly sedated and will remain that way as a precaution. But if required, this will allow you to completely incapacitate him.'

The inhibitor bracelet dangled from Blake's fingers. Kira hauled herself up onto the kitchen bench, bare feet swinging against the cupboard doors. 'I know this isn't a joke, 'cause you are physically incapable of humour,' Kira said. 'But, B, what the hell is going on?'

Blake rubbed at a damp fleck of alcohol on her chin, staring down at a crack in the tiled floor. The ultimate question.

One she'd blinded herself to for far too long. 'I need him out there for just a couple of hours. Enough time to assess reactions, both from Azrael and from the people he interacts with. The data will be useful when completing the others.'

The lie fell with greater ease than she'd anticipated. Perhaps because its roots were in truth. But she did not want to merely observe Azrael. She wanted to conceal him. The heightened sense of urgency, the near-manic energy that had gripped Captain Nex and the Syranians the past couple of days, and Tamas's sudden desire to distance himself from her, had dissolved Blake's focus on the technology. On the marvel of creation.

As the side-effects of the Waters running through her body heightened, so did her paranoia. The terrible grip of doubt was suffocating.

'Others?' Kira frowned. 'You're building more robo-boys?'

'Yes.'

'Why? Are they building an army down there? Are Captain Asshat and his merry band about to take over the world?' Kira smirked, setting off a dimple high in her left cheek.

Until that moment Blake had been satisfied with her ready answers, her self-assured half truths. Yet now the single word required to answer stuck to the back of her throat.

'No.' Blake forced it free, but her uncertainty cracked her voice. Four hunters, searching for a sole target. That was what Tamas had told her. In the beginning. When she cared little for whatever games the aliens wished to play. In a world populated with billions, what were four hunters and one singular goal?

Kira was silent, her focus on the inhibitor bracelet. She lifted it from where it swayed on Blake's fingertips and slipped it over her wrist.

'Are they done?' An uneasy note clung to her words.

Blake watched her sister. 'Done?'

'Going? Adios? Sayonara, goodbye. Leaving.'

'Why are you raising your voice?'

'Why aren't you answering the fucking question. Are the aliens leaving?'

'No. Why would that –' Blake's confusion made her pause. Then all at once it dawned on her. Eron. 'No. They are not leaving.'

Rossiter had insisted Kira still nursed an emotional connection to the disgraced alien, despite the chaos the interlude had caused and Kira's flippant dismissal of events. Blake had witnessed a hint of it herself when she took them both to see Azrael, but she did not realise quite how deep the connection ran until now. 'Kira, we do not have time to further this discussion. Gwen is waiting. You need to meet her, now. And this must stay classified.'

She grasped Azrael's shoulder, intending to assist him to his feet, but the gallu jerked at her touch. Blake released her hold.

'I've got him,' Kira said. 'Just calm your tits. I can't go out on your stupid mission looking like this.'

She shrugged off her nightshirt, standing bare-breasted while choosing a shirt from a pile of laundered clothes sitting in a basket on the far side of the dining table. A marking between her small breasts caught Blake's eye.

'When did you get that?' The sight of the surgical wound gave Blake the usual turn of stomach, but the artwork that had been worked over it was actually quite beautiful: an intricate kaleidoscope of blue butterflies, running half the length of her considerable scar.

'It's called a tat, Grandma B. And I got it ages ago.' Kira pulled on a bra, then a long-sleeved black top, covering the tattoo. 'Blame Eron. He was being a pussy and wouldn't get one. So I went first.'

She slid a white skull-print cardigan over the shirt.

'The Syranian got a tattoo?' Blake's concern eased. Kira may be careless, and irresponsible, but her ability to influence those around her was unsurpassed. And Eron had come to no harm in her care. Had remained undiscovered despite both Kira's and his own severe intoxication.

'He did. A dog's paw.' Kira zipped up a pair of black leather pants and tugged on sneakers. A skull-print pattern adorned the well-worn shoes as well. Rossiter, noting Kira's preoccupation with skulls, had purchased them on Blake's behalf when her work prevented her from allocating time to birthdays. 'So where am I supposed to go with Mr Chatty?'

'The Wheel and Barrow. It is quiet on a Tuesday evening, I believe. Gwen is waiting with a vehicle at the East Exit. She has already cleared your exit.'

One advantage of her status was the effect it had on those around her. The requests of the woman deemed responsible for the economic success of the Facility were usually met with hurried, breathless compliance.

'You know the name of my pub? You're full of surprises tonight.' Kira crouched beside Azrael, whose concentration had not wavered from the TV during the entire conversation. She looped her flesh arm through his. 'Come on, big guy, we've got a hot date.'

He did not look at her as he allowed her to help him to his feet, all the while still mesmerised by a car commercial. A dance of nerves erupted beneath Blake's skin at the thought of discovering exactly what Azrael was, what her carapace contained. She opened the front door, standing behind it to stay out of view of anyone passing by outside. 'You have your cell phone, I assume?'

Kira nodded, black curls bobbing. 'Sure do, Secret Squirrel. Ready to complete the mission. Wait, hang on a second, how the fuck do you know the Wheel and Barrow is quiet on a Tuesday night? Tell me it's not the same way you knew I was in Greece last year.'

'Just go, Kira.' This had taken too long. Her absence from the lower levels could not be hidden forever by Rossiter.

'Not going to fucking happen.'

Kira stood just inside the threshold with Azrael on her arm. He twisted his head, trying to keep a view of the TV. And Kira made no attempt to move, her expression defiant.

Blake gave in. 'I have access to the surveillance equipment in the Wheel and Barrow. I understand you think that's wrong, but it's a security measure to protect the Facility. A precaution. Alcohol loosens tongues, and we can ascertain what, if any, classified information is leaking out into the public arena.'

'What information did you need when you watched me having sex by the pool?'

'I told you. Just your whereabouts. The viewing was as

unfortunate for our tech as it was for you. I can assure you.'

'I can assure you, you are fucked up. Most sisters just call if they want to know where you are.'

'Kira, stop. I need your help.' Blake clutched the door hard. 'Can you just do this, no smart mouth? No bullshit?'

She braced for the inevitable retort, but it didn't come. Kira stepped up close. Far too close.

'I'll do it because I think you are losing your shit,' she said softly. 'And anything that might piss off Captain Nex and Tamas is high on my to-do list. But promise me you will never, ever dress an android in our dad's stuff again, Blake, and we are good.' Kira nodded at the sneakers on Az's feet. Scuffed black running shoes with a faded orange symbol on the heels. 'You said you threw out all his things.'

An odd prickling teased the backs of Blake's eyes. 'Those shoes are all I retained. Just go, Kira. I'll call you. Don't forget to take the faux skin for your arm.'

Blake kept her gaze lifted, focused on her sister. Concealing the limb that had made Kira, and indeed herself, a B-grade celebrity was certainly prudent. If this went as Blake intended, they would not remain at the Wheel and Barrow.

'Blake, I'm sorry you're hurting so much. You need to –
'

'Go!' Blake shouted. Azrael jerked against Kira's hold.

'Go, Kira.'

Anger brightened Kira's amber eyes. 'And they say I'm the messed-up one. Fuck you, Blake. We're gone.'

She slammed the door, and the prints hanging either side shuddered against the wall. Blake slid to her knees, resting her head against the cool wood. It was done. She curled her trembling hands against her chest and waited for the panic to subside.

'Go, Kira.'

KIRA - 10

Kira knew better than to stare at the steering wheel. It always made her want to heave, watching the smooth leather rotate back and forth as the automated car navigated its way to a destination. Her guts were saying, *look away*, but her head was too busy trying to work out her sister's deal. True to Blake's word, Gwen the wonder tech had met them and herded both Kira and Az into the vehicle, waving them past security after a few words to the guards. Kira dragged her gaze from the shifting wheel and up to the rearview mirror. Azrael still lay where he'd fallen, draped across the back seat like some Roman emperor, knees up, one arm resting in the footwell. His hoodie rode up, pulling the white T-shirt beneath with it, exposing his honey-coloured belly. The view was, admittedly, not terrible.

'She's lost it. My sister is certified.' Kira sat in the front passenger seat, sneakers kicked off, bare feet up on the dash.

'Did you see her face? Looked like the fucking hounds of hell were chasing her. The girl who doesn't flinch in thunderstorms, didn't bat an eyelid when that earthquake hit last year, is flipping out over you.'

For most of the twenty-minute journey, Az had stared at the ceiling as though its beige surface were the roof of the goddamn Sistine Chapel.

'I feel like I should feed you grapes or something. Sit up, dude.' She swivelled in her seat, reaching for him, aiming for his exposed skin. Couldn't help herself. Those stomach curves looked as though they'd feel velvety. She loved velvet. Her metal fingertips found faux skin.

'Oh shit.'

Contact was deliciously unpleasant, like hot wax on bare skin, before it jolted into something not so great — a shock of electricity shooting up her arm, and a blurring in her vision. Kira ripped her hand away, settling back on her haunches. Azrael sat bolt upright, his head knocking the roof.

'What the fucking hell was that shit?' Kira shook her metal limb. It tingled. No. Not tingled. It vibrated. Hummed like a dildo on low speed. 'Okay. Weirdness has gone to defcon five. What did you just do, robo-boy?'

She pressed her arm against her belly, her breathing coming in short intakes. Though the vibrating thing was disconcerting, it wasn't exactly awful.

Azrael did his usual thing, he stared. Only this time it wasn't the vacant newborn look. His expression was soft and settled, as if for once he weren't trying to peer into shadow. Kira leaned forward, holding her breath. The emerald-green of his eyes was impossibly vibrant. Tiny rust-coloured specks floated in the green pools, giving them a depth good enough to dive into.

Jesus, she wanted to dive in. Sink down and drown.

Azrael leaned forward to meet her, and Kira's own reflection shimmered in his eyes. Her lungs ached with the need to breathe, but that could wait. Everything could wait. The world was waiting. Perfectly still.

Something flickered in the depths of the tiny emerald lakes, a shadow passing beneath the surface. The car stopped dead. Kira gasped as the jolt pushed her back. Away from Azrael.

'Okay.' She squinted against the sudden dullness of the car's interior. 'That happened.'

What the hell was *that*? She needed a cigarette and a lie down. The vibration in her arm was gone. Kira tugged at her cardigan, glancing down. She wouldn't have been surprised to see her tits hanging out; the contact had smashed into her like a one-night stand in a nightclub toilet. But she was fully clothed.

An odd sense of relief filled her. Az was beautiful, no doubt, and something freaky had just happened, but getting wet in the panties over it felt all kinds of wrong.

He was a hot lump of dumb again. Mouth open, eyes vacant again. Slumped against the back seat. If he drooled, it wouldn't surprise her.

'God, what is going on, Blake?'

She glanced at the wristband. Sending a mute, catatonic robo-boy out into the world with her pisshead sister wasn't Blake's usual MO. She craved control the way most people craved chocolate or heroin. Something was up in the Facility. Very high up. Granted, Kira had been quite adept at blending Eron in, if she did say so herself, but Eron was different. The guy could wipe his own ass. And though he had stunning eyes – if white eyeballs were your thing, which it turned out, for her, they were, who knew? – nothing hid in the depths of them. Or rose to the surface like a miniature aurora borealis.

'So, mental note.' Kira cleared her throat. 'My metal and your metal, not such a good combination.'

Fucking great combination actually. But she couldn't sit in the pub touching up the mute, getting her kicks. She'd have to make sure it was flesh hand only for contact. 'We're going in there, okay?' She nodded at the faded red door. The car had parked them in the alleyway alongside the pub, beside the staff entrance. Cat piss and rotten vegetables scented the air. 'You ready?'

Getting Az out of the car was surprisingly easy. He mimicked her. Right down to the overhead arm stretch she did when she stood up. Then things got adorable. Azrael ran his hand over the brick wall, fingers tracing the graffiti there.

'First time seeing brick, huh? Always a memorable moment.' Kira stood at the door. She should herd him inside, but it was too precious. He moved on to one of the dumpsters. Put both hands on it, moving along the side as though he were reading some kind of braille on the smooth metal. An old, disturbingly-stained mattress hung over the far edge. He made a beeline for it, and Kira considered stopping him for all of two seconds but watching him sniff the grotty fabric was amusing. And there'd been far too little amusement lately. The guy was all goggle-eyed and entranced, like a kid seeing snow for the first time.

'You think that smells good, wait till you smell the inside of the Barrow,' she said. 'Beer-soaked carpet and toilets that will make your eyes water. But the vodka is good, and the curry divine. Let's go.'

Two hours in, everything was going well. As well as could be expected when babysitting a giant child. At just after nine on a Tuesday night, the pub had barely a dozen people in it. Mostly regulars. Most of them beyond bored with Kira's ever-changing assortment of sidekicks, and after the initial interest when Kira had walked in, they'd all gone back to their beer and fish curries. Surprisingly, no one had complained yet about Perry's music choice. K-pop tunes thudded through the speakers, loud enough to force everyone to yell-speak at their companions.

Perry let the last few drops from a Moet bottle drip into a flute and handed it to Kira. 'It is good to see your ugly mug again, K.'

'Ditto, my friend. Forgot how damn huge your nose was.'

Perry blew her a kiss. Kira feigned catching it and snorting it off the wooden bar top.

'Sweetie,' Perry said, 'your new little friend is delightful, but whatever happened to that tall, lean piece you brought in a couple of times? One with the silver hair and lips like a slice of heaven?' He threw the empty Moet with well-practised aim into a bin at the far end of the bar, where it joined the other bottle Kira had sucked back since they'd arrived. 'Alice, go grab some more of those from the storeroom, will you?' Perry called to the redhead clearing tables.

She nodded, balancing an impressive pile of stacked plates against equally impressive breasts.

Kira dipped her finger into the foam settling in her glass. To be fair, the first bottle was only half-full when she'd arrived. Someone else this evening had an appetite for expensive champagne.

'Meh.' She shrugged off mention of Eron as if he were a fly settling on her. 'Got bored with him. He wouldn't put out.'

Perry scratched at the short-trimmed beard covering his chin. 'Sweetheart, please. We've known each other too long. Occasionally, you dive a little too deep into someone, and that's about the time you start fucking around. Booking in Liam till the poor guy's dick is ready to fall off. That's pretty much been your last couple of months. Hell, you left the country. Then you're back for a week or two and you disappear again. Must have been love if Kira is on the run. And no prizes for guessing it was you who fucked up the happy-ever-after.'

'Christ almighty, stick to sucking balls. It's what you do best. You're a shitty counsellor.' Kira turned her back to her friend, leaning against the bar. She winced, remembering too late the bruise on her back where Blake had shoved her against the kitchen sink.

'That's why we get along so well, my dear. Shared talents.' A soft whipping sound followed, and something snapped at her flesh arm. She turned to see Perry sauntering away, waving the black tea towel he'd just flicked at her like a victor's flag, his pearly whites made even more luminous by the rich, deep shade of his skin. 'You can pay for that shit he's wasting, by the way.'

He gestured towards the booth where Azrael sat pulling out each and every paper napkin from the dispenser, arranging them in a warped kind of snowflake design on the table. A woman stood at the end of the table, wobbling back and forth, a half-empty pint of golden goodness in her hands. She'd come into the pub about an hour after Kira and Azrael. Kind of hard to miss.

Oompa Loompas had died and she'd bathed in their blood apparently. She was as orange as, well, an orange. The tan queen had spindly short legs and a shock of white hair that eclipsed Kira's in the messy stakes. It might have been a bob once; now it was a bird's-nest. A nest for bower birds apparently, the ones that collected shiny things. An assortment of clips and ribbons clung to random strands. The woman was way too interested in Azrael's attempts at artistry.

'That's so beautiful,' she of the dead Oompa Loompas declared, loud enough for some other patrons to glance her way.

'Oh fuck.' Kira sighed.

'Quick, sweetie,' Perry laughed, 'she's moving in on

your territory.'

Kira flicked him the bird. 'Do something useful, like change that fucking music.'

She strode towards the table, champagne safe in metal clutches. 'Okay, show's over, love. I need to talk with my man here. Private stuff.'

Tan Queen turned towards her, stumbling against the edge of the table. Azrael glanced up, but his jade-greens didn't so much as flicker over the orange catastrophe in front of him. It was all about Kira. His eyes locked on her like heat-seeking missiles. Even the drunken mess seemed to notice. Dark brown eyes darted between Kira and Azrael, flicking back and forth as if she were watching a tennis match. The chick was older than Kira had first thought. A roadmap of wrinkles made their way through the orange wasteland, but she wasn't as unattractive as her hair. An old-lady stateliness was draped about her, her rouged cheeks resting around a smiling mouth.

'Lady, please. Leave us alone.' Kira swept her hand towards a couple of empty tables at the room's centre. 'Plenty of spare seats. You don't need this one.'

The smile faded. 'No need to be so harsh. Just being friendly.' She lifted one hand from the table to point at Azrael, and the movement made her rock. 'He all right?'

'Perfectly fine.' Kira took the woman's arm. 'Go on, get

yourself another drink or something.'

A hint of spices wafted off the woman. Cinnamon or allspice or something else that should be in a bakery.

'Righto, righto. No need to manhandle me, girlie.' Tan Queen tugged her arm free of Kira's grip with a strength that didn't match her scrawny frame. 'I'm leaving.'

The woman studied Kira, her gaze dropping to her metal limb, then dragging itself up the length of the armadillo, as if she were counting each layer and saving it to memory.

'Want to take a picture? It will last longer,' Kira said. An oldie, but still a damn goodie. 'Piss off, now.' She flicked her metal fingers in that condescending way asshole villains did in movies. But Tan Queen was too busy staring at Kira's hand to appreciate the Academy Award moment. She darted another look at Azrael, raised her beer to him, and then stumbled away, snaking her way across the crimson, leaf-patterned carpet, her skin colour clashing with it in a gut-wrenching way.

Kira snatched the napkin dispenser from Azrael. 'No more masterpieces, my friend. Too many trees died for the honour of being wiped across someone's ketchup-soaked lips.'

Azrael stared down at the deep brown table, fingers tracing the veins in the wood. Any second now dribble would run from his mouth. She stuffed a couple of napkins in her pocket and dumped the rest on the neighbouring empty table.

'I'm fucking starving. How about we –' Kira jerked at the sudden vibration against her hip. Scrambling to pull her phone from her slim-fitting pant pocket, Kira almost dropped it in her haste to get it to her ear. 'Blake? About fucking time. Jesus, what is the –'

'Kira, it's time to go. Now.'

'Go where?'

'Leave the pub.' Blake's voice rose over the music. 'I want you to take Azrael. I need you to keep him hidden until this is . . . Kira can you hear me? That music is terribly loud.'

'Heard you, yes, understood you, no. Keep him hidden? Hidden from Captain Asshat? B, did you finally smoke that weed I gave you? I reckon it's probably stale as shit by now. Maybe go easy.'

'Pay attention, Kira. The quicker we make this, the better,' Blake said. 'You need to leave there but not in the car you arrived in. I'm going to set the auto to head out of Pryden, maybe into Lorhurst. Are there any clubs there that you go to? Somewhere they'd expect you to go?'

'There's not even a Girl Scout clubhouse in Lorhurst. No. I do not go there. Blake. Seriously, you are not James Bond. Not even close. Tell me what the fuck is happening.'

Long pause. So long Kira held the phone away from her ear to check the signal hadn't been lost. 'Blake?'

'I can't tell you what is happening. I'm not entirely sure myself.'

Kira's grip on the phone tightened. 'Blake Beckworth uncertain? Then it's the fucking apocalypse.' She laughed, short and sweet, and took another swig of her champagne, watching Azrael dip a fingertip into a blob of ketchup clinging to the top of the squeeze bottle. Blake's silence seemed to press on the room. Even the K-pop boys toned down their screeching.

Finally, 'I'm asking you to exercise your talent for running away, Kira.'

'Insulting a person is generally not the best way to get them to help you.'

'It is not an insult. Do not take this phone with you. Leave it at the bar. Have Perry take you to the private airport on Lancaster Road. An aircraft is waiting for you. Say nothing to your friend of any of this. Have him believe you are simply leaving town. Again.'

Azrael sniffed the tabletop. Kira glanced around the room. No one paid them any attention. Even the tan queen was preoccupied at the bar, sitting on a stool, shoving French fries into her mouth, drinking a freshly filled beer. Perry held up another bottle of Moët, brandishing it at Kira. She nodded and gave him a thumbs-up. Fuck yes, she needed another one.

'A plane? Exactly how far am I taking the robot?'

Another one of those long, weird pauses but this time she could hear her sister breathing. Long inhales and exhales.

'There is money on the plane, cash. Use it for whatever you need.'

'What do I need? I mean does he need nappies? Do I sing him to sleep at night?'

Blake laughed. A knot coiled in Kira's gut. Blake was not okay.

'You just need to keep him away from here,' Blake said. 'For a while. Promise me you will say nothing to Perry. I understand there is a strong friendship between you.'

Holy shitballs, had Blake just sounded melancholy? Kira pressed the phone against her ear. This was kind of fucking delicious. Blake had gone rogue, and she needed her help. Kira didn't even give a shit why. Pathetic as it was, and damn, it was pathetic, Kira was getting off on being back on Blake's radar of fucks given.

'Haven't told him about the aliens in the basement, your secret is safe with me.' Always had been. Just in case Blake ever bothered to notice. 'I'm not even sure what the secret is, so I think we're all good. So where's the plane taking us?'

Honestly, this day was turning into the best fucking thing ever. Late-night flights to nowhere, hauling a stolen piece of tech that was probably worth more than the military's entire manifest. A piece of tech that was rubbing ketchup on his lip as if it were a new lipstick shade.

'The pilot has destination information,' Blake said. 'You'll understand when you land. Just do what you do, but do it right now. Keep him away from here. No matter what you might hear. Understand? Leave now.'

And she ended the call. Just hung up the damn thing without waiting to see if Kira understood. Which she didn't. Not in the slightest. Kira stared down at the blank screen. Perry's arrival went unnoticed until he was right beside her. Drink in hand.

He handed it to her. 'That didn't look pleasant. Everything okay?' Perry pulled something from his pocket. The faux skin for Kira's arm. 'Found it in the alleyway beside your car when I took out some trash. What did you and your special friend get up to out there?'

'Wouldn't you like to know?'

Perry raised a dark eyebrow. 'Considering your friend doesn't look like he knows what his hands are for, let alone his dick, yes – kind of. Can he even understand English?'

'Enough. He's not from around here, clearly. I'm just making sure he has a good time while he visits.'

Kira took the sleeve. It was, admittedly, bloody good. Freckles, veins, light hairs all so in sync with Kira's real arm that it would take some very up-close-and-personal scrutiny to pick the deception. She hardly ever wore it; it felt too much like wearing a lie. Tonight though, the faux skin was perfect. She slid it over the armadillo, and it rolled into place as though it had a life of its own.

'Perry, I need a favour. I need a lift to the airport.' When his deep browns rolled, Kira cupped Perry's face in her hands. 'I swear I'll work a week straight when I get back. You'll be free as a bird. But I gotta get out of here.'

'Again? You just got back.'

'I've been back a couple of weeks. What do you want from me?'

Perry grasped her wrists gently and tugged her hands from his face. 'K, I know your dad's birthday is coming up real soon –'

Snatching her hands free, Kira took a step away from her friend. 'What the fuck has that got to do with anything?'

Christ. Right in the jugular. The room tilted. Of course she knew when her dad's goddamn birthday was. It was like the black hole of dates. Dragging every other day towards it. The only day with a stronger gravitational pull was the day she had fucking killed him. Last day of stone-cold sobriety.

'Everything, maybe?' Perry shrugged, clasping his hands to his chest. 'K, I'm sorry, but I gotta say something. When did you and Blake last spend it together? Any birthday for that matter?'

'Perry, take me to the airport.' Before she did something she regretted. Like smash her glass in his concerned, caring face. 'Like right now.'

A sudden break in the music draped the moment in odd silence. Perry's dark eyebrows knitted together, and she thought for a moment he might refuse. If he said one more word about her shitty handling of grief, she was going to lose it. The dude had just crapped all over her happy place. Till now, she'd gone more than five minutes without thinking about her fucking dad.

'K, I'm sorry. I didn't mean to piss you off. You know I love you, right?'

'We're good. All good.' Smile, damn it. Smile so bright your cheeks crack. 'Airport?'

'Sure. Yep. Give me five and I'll get Alice to handle the bar.'

KIRA - 11

Kira ran her thumb over the digital dial on the inhibitor bracelet, lowering the level by one more notch. Nothing screeched at her, no flashing red lights or anything, so that had to be a good sign. It had taken way too long to get robo-boy in behind the bar and halfway down the hallway.

'Okay, how about that?'

Unsurprisingly, there was no answer. But Az did lift his head higher and didn't lean quite so hard. Kira adjusted her hold around him. Her flesh arm wrapped around a waist narrower than hers and as solid as a pillar of marble. 'Right, let's do this.'

They passed through the storage room and past the gag-inducing odour of the staff toilet. Despite there being plenty of room in the hallway to walk side by side, Az's hip pressed against hers as though they were magnetised. When they were almost at the back door, he lifted his hand, planting it over her flesh hand where it gripped his hip.

'Oh no.' Kira tried to pull away, bracing for the flip-out. 'Not a good idea.'

But the mini hysterics were a waste of time. Nothing, not even a spark this time. Azrael intertwined his slender fingers with her chubbier digits. No pain. Just warm skin. So the armadillo was some kind of conductor? Didn't seem such a crazy idea, considering the metal hadn't exactly been dug out of the nearest quarry. Azrael leaned into her. It was like being nudged by a brick wall. The guy was nothing if not solid. Kira tried to pull her hand free to open the back door, but Azrael wasn't letting go anytime soon. She tried once more, gave up, and used her left arm to open the door and pull forward. Azrael planted himself on the spot like a pretty tree.

'Door open, means walk through.' Kira strained against him. 'Basic exiting one-oh-one.'

The temperature had slipped way down, the desert showing off its flexibility with a chilling flourish that swept through the open doorway. Her black leather pants were cutting it, but the twins were on high alert beneath the press of her 'bandage' wrap top. Perry's car, a midsized SUV, was only a short distance down the alleyway, its ridiculously bright yellow body paint glowing in the dark. One step at a time, she coaxed

Azrael down the three steps. He wasn't coming easily. He didn't say a thing – that would have just been weird – but it looked an awful lot as if he were shitting his pants. Kira considered downing the tranqs again; surely the thing would scream at her if she went too far.

'Not sure what you've got to be scared about, dude.' Kira grunted, muscles in her shoulder protesting as she pushed Az forward. 'But this is going to be the longest night in the world if you are going to take this long to do anything.'

Finally, sweet Jesus finally, he hit ground level and released the grip on her hand. Kira pulled her arm free, shaking her numb fingers. 'Well, aren't you so brave. Those nasty steps didn't stand a chance.'

The door, slow as all hell to close behind them, did so now with a firm clunk. Azrael froze, unmoving as the mannequin he resembled. The single light in the alleyway was pathetically dull, and shadows hugged everything in the narrow passageway.

'Okay,' Kira said. 'You can do this, big, brave, silent one. Almost there. We're going to get in that car there, see?'

She turned to point out the car and jabbed her finger into the soft, squishy cheek of Tan Queen. 'Jesus fucking Christ, are you insane?'

'Sorry, sorry.' The woman rubbed at her cheek, her

stark-white hair like a ghost floating above her head. 'I wasn't sneaking up on you. I thought –'

'Go away. Just go the hell away, woman.'

Tan Queen muttered something, and before Kira could tell her to piss off again, she dashed right past her.

'Hey, what the fuck?' Kira shouted.

The woman made a beeline for Azrael, and without so much as a how-do-you-do, she pushed up on her tiptoes and planted her hands squarely on Az's chest. There was a weird frozen moment. No one moved. No one said a word. Then the sad alleyway light called it a day. Glass exploded, tinkling onto the ground. At the same moment, as if she'd been hit by flying shrapnel, the woman dropped. Heavy as a sack of potatoes, ass-first to the ground, flopping onto her back, skull meeting road with a cringe-inducing crack.

Azrael staggered back, his fingers curled into claws. His mouth working open and shut as though he wanted to heave.

'Shit,' Kira said. 'What the hell?'

She crouched down beside the woman. Only the half-moon threw any light on the alleyway now, illuminating the tan queen's white mop of hair. She groaned, her breathing rapid, as if she'd just finished a run. But alive.

'Okay,' Kira said. 'Not dead.'

She glanced up. Azrael's line of sight was fixed on the

prone woman. He raked his fingers down his arm, his head working back and forth as if he were Stevie Wonder belting out a tune.

'Oh no, no, buddy. Not now.' Kira approached him slowly, hands raised. Totally not the time for a panic attack. 'Look at me. It's okay. She's okay. Oompa Loompa lady shouldn't have touched you. I know.'

Back and forth, back and forth, he rocked his upper body. Hands clutched to his midriff, shoulders hunched forward. Kira had seen it all before, but before there had been a solid panel of glass between them. Something that would come in very handy if he started to lash out.

'Look at me, Az, not her. Hey, do you remember the video I showed you, where the cat is playing chopsticks with the chopsticks?' She laughed, strained and humourless. 'Like, it's funny 'cause the song is called "Chopsticks", but that's what the cat is —'

Light spilled across the scene.

'Everything okay out here?' Perry stepped through the open doorway, spotting the fallen woman. 'What the hell happened?'

Kira hesitated, her attention all on Azrael. Light from inside the pub pooled around him. He'd stopped rocking, and his arms rested at his sides. His focus lifted from the woman and moved to the slowly closing door. Azrael lifted his hand, tilting it back and forth as if it was the very first time he'd noticed it stuck to the end of his arm.

'Kira, what is going on?' Perry rushed past her, reaching the woman in three long strides.

'She was like this when we came out.' Kira grabbed at all the straws available to her. 'Azrael got a little freaked about it. Don't think he's seen a rotten drunk before.'

If she did say so herself, it was a magnificent display of thinking on one's feet. Only a fraction of it was actually a lie.

'Oh man, I'm going to call an ambulance.' Perry grimaced. 'This woman's been hanging around here a lot lately, but this is the first time I've seen her legless. I'm going to take her inside. Your ride will have to wait.'

'Can I have the keys?' Kira said. 'I'll let you do the Good Samaritan thing, and we'll wait in the car.'

Perry tossed her the car keys and bent down to pick up the woman. She was short and could have done with a decent sandwich or two, so he managed easily. 'Don't do anything in my car I wouldn't do.'

'That ship sailed a year ago.'

Kira held the door open for Perry so he could manoeuvre the woman inside. Her hair was a little messier, if that was possible, but she had no scratches, cuts, or gaping wounds. No bloody injuries. In Kira's expert medical opinion, she'd be okay once she came to. The whole thing just a warped, drunken hallucination. Kira grabbed Azrael's arm, tugging a couple of times before he left the circle of light. His drool face was back, and he stared down at the golden glow on the pavement as if it were a long-lost lover.

Kira guided him to the car. Not so difficult this time. The dude was as keen to get out of there as Kira was. 'Little over-reaction there buddy.'

Going on the run was one thing, leaving people in unconscious piles was another altogether. She couldn't keep attention away from him if he kept flooring people. For the first time since Blake had shooed them out of the Facility, Kira had some doubts.

Getting Azrael back into the car was surprisingly easy. Maybe the dude was still in shock, maybe he thought the darkness wouldn't get him in there. Whatever the reason, he hopped in as though he'd been getting into cars forever. He huddled into the corner, sitting at an angle that pressed his butt against the closed door, clutching at the back seat as if the whole car were about to shoot up into space. Not an intimidating sight. But the rocking and scratching had stopped. Good thing.

Kira sighed, wishing she'd brought a drink for the road.

'Shit, what have I gotten myself into?'

Azrael's hand was on her metal fingers before she took another breath. Contact was all hot wax on bare skin again, tingling nerves and hollow stomach. Pleasurable pain. Then came the jolt. A sharp snap of electricity crackled between the metals, and dropped to an uncomfortably pleasant tingle. The whole armadillo hummed beneath the faux skin, the echo of it playing with every nerve in Kira's body. A groan lolled at the back of her throat, and her eyelids fluttered low.

Azrael didn't want to go back. He really, really didn't want to go back to the Facility.

The groan wedged itself halfway up her throat. She was afraid. No. Kira frowned. She wasn't afraid at all.

He was. Terrified.

The fear weaved through her, coarse and vibrant.

Kira jerked her hand free, and the groan caught in her throat morphed into a cry. Eyes wide open, she met Azrael's steady emerald gaze.

'Az, you poor bastard,' she whispered.

He was alive in there. She'd felt him there, buried beneath the metalwork. Kira flexed her metal fingertips. They were still tingling. The whole limb was too-near-the-campfire warm. Holy shitballs. If she wasn't very much mistaken, she'd just slam-dunked into Azrael's psyche. A living, pulsing thing.

The dude wasn't a robot. Not even close. Fucking hell, Blake. Azrael still watched her. Whatever it was behind those eyes, watched her. Maybe she should be shitting herself, but the only one doing that right now was Az. And the idea of that pissed her off. Way more than it should do.

'I hate that fucking place too,' Kira said, voice raspy. 'You're not going back there.'

For the time being, they would play Blake's game. Azrael slumped back against the seat, chin dropping to his chest. Kira didn't have the advantage of a hot-and-heavy connection this time, but she was going to go out on a limb and say he looked relaxed.

A few minutes later, Azrael appeared to have drifted off to sleep. Eyes closed. His posture a little awkward, like a toddler who'd just fallen asleep halfway through playing. Completely damn adorable. And if anyone came near the guy, she'd cut them. Kira shook her head, dislodging the sudden thought. For fuck's sake, what had been in that champagne? She shifted out of the back seat and hopped into the passenger seat, needing to put a little distance between them.

Perry returned about fifteen minutes later. He climbed into the driver's seat and started the car. 'All good here?'

Peachy. 'Yeah. All good.' She massaged her bare feet, boots and socks discarded in the footwell. 'How's the patient?'

'She's going to feel like hell tomorrow. Wasted off her tits. And she's got a great bump on the head. They're taking her away now, but she's not too happy about it.'

So it really was all good. No permanent damage to anyone. Nothing to see here. Everyone move along. Kira danced her feet against the mat in the footwell.

'So where are we going?' Perry revved the engine a couple of times, and the car tried to rattle its exhaust pipe loose.

'If you think we can make it, the airport on Lancaster.'

'Is he attracted to your smart mouth?' Perry nodded his head at Azrael.

'Of course. Can't get enough of my mouth in general.'

'Where you guys flying to?'

'Good question,' Kira replied and changed the topic, quizzing Perry about his lack of love or sex life. The discussion, mostly Perry telling her not to be a bitch, killed the next twenty minutes of driving.

Then she was air-kissing her bestie and waving sweet goodbye. 'Bye bye, bitch.'

'Later, slut.' Perry blew her a kiss, wearing a grin from ear to ear. 'Miss you already.'

As his car roared to life, and there was no chance he'd hear, Kira replied, 'You too.'

Goodbyes should be illegal. They were hazardous to health.

A perfectly coiffed cabin attendant guided them onto the snow-white private jet, handing Kira a whisky and milk after she took her seat. Giving the girl a smile that usually parted legs, Kira nodded to the cockpit.

'So, I love surprises and all, but now that we're on board can you fill me in? Where are we off to?'

Warm brown eyes bright, the girl smiled back at her. 'Bankston Airport, about three hours flight. Do you know it?'

Kira shook her head.

'It's a small regional airport between Beleiro and Melgrove.'

The smile slipped from Kira's face. 'Okay, thanks.'

The attendant backed off, muttering something about readying the cabin for takeoff, leaving Kira alone with a bunch of angry, churning thoughts. Beleiro was a bawdy, overelectrified casino town Kira knew well, but it was the much smaller town of Melgrove that made her stomach churn. Kira stared down at the shoes Blake had put on Azrael. Blake had walked out halfway through their dad's funeral declaring herself too occupied with putting Kira back together again to waste time with mourning. She'd barely mentioned their father since. Now all this. The shoes and the town of Melgrove. The backwater town with great fishing and even better pubs, where they were supposed to have had a weekend away to celebrate Kira's twenty-first. But Blake had been MIA on that trip, too busy working at the Facility to join Kira and their dad. Just as she had been a year later. Too caught up to go to dinner the night a blown tyre and a fucking great tree had ripped a hole in their lives.

The attendant offered Azrael a blanket. He stared at her like she'd offered to castrate him.

'He's fine. I'll take it though.' Kira spread the white cashmere over her knees, nestling into the cushy leather seat, the heat of the whisky blooming in her stomach. Kira drained the glass. Azrael was transfixed by the view through the window. The attendant refilled Kira's empty glass without a word, and in one gulp it was gone, too. Azrael had better be worth it. Their father was so damn proud of anything his eldest child did, Blake could have shit on his birthday cake and he'd have clapped his hands and said how wonderful it was. He'd had no idea of the scope of what went on at the Facility. No idea about the aliens in the basement. Blake had only brought Kira into the fold after the accident. Like doing the big reveal somehow made it all better. Negated the fact that Kira wouldn't have been driving at all if Blake had gone to pick up their dad from the station like she'd promised.

Blake was messed up. That wasn't news. Bottled up everything till it blocked her up like an enormous grief turd. And constipation at that level clearly did fucky things to a person. Case in point, part-man, part-android, part-who-knows-fucking-what sitting opposite.

Kira would stay on the ride. For now. For the poor son of a bitch caught up in this. But if Blake thought she would sit with ghosts in Melgrove, then she could go fuck herself.

BLAKE - 12

Blake watched the recording for a third time. Perry wiped down the bar, one, two, three swipes with a chequered cloth whose colour was hidden from her in the black-and-white footage. He pulled a tray of steaming glasses from a dishwasher at one end of the bar, leaning his face over the rising heat and eyes fluttering closed. Only to open again almost immediately.

'Hello?' he called, moving out from behind the bar and heading into the main area. 'You shouldn't be in here, get the hell out.'

But his confused expression belied his authoritative voice. He could hear someone but clearly couldn't see them. Perry twisted towards a loud crash at his right, then just as swiftly had to swing the other way when a mirroring sound occurred out of sight of the camera to his left.

Blake had played the recording over and over. Each

movement was seared into her memory. Five hours after Perry had delivered Azrael and Kira to the airport, he lay motionless on the red-carpeted floor of the bar. In all likelihood he was deceased. Yet Blake could not find the impetus to abandon her surveillance just yet.

'Shit.' She bit into her knuckle, eyes darting between the live feed on the left-hand screen and the earlier recorded vision on her right. Blood warmed her lips as her teeth pierced thin skin. 'Come on, get up. Get up, Perry.'

The man had lain still for almost fifteen minutes now, and still indecision gripped her. Drawing any attention to this event could lead to Azrael's absence being discovered faster than it would have otherwise.

The door to the basement swung open, and Blake's heart slammed into her ribcage. Rossiter raced down the short flight of stairs, his heavy body thunderous against the wooden slats. 'What's wrong? Are you all right?'

'I would prefer that you announced yourself before making your way into my basement.'

The bald-headed man paused at the base of the stairs, his face dark with irritation. 'And I would prefer that you do not summon me urgently without giving any indication of your status.'

'The issue is external. Not with me.'

Her status was nauseated. Her fingers were twitching as though the nerves had taken a life of their own. Her pulse thudded at her temples. It was three thirty in the morning. Apart from the solitary hour of sleep she'd woken from a short time ago, she'd been awake for approximately thirty-six hours. An unreasonable length of time, even by her standards, but Tamas and Captain Nex had been relentless in ensuring all testing on the four carapaces was complete before they removed—tore— them from her care.

Blake rubbed at the grooves marked into her cheek where it had rested against the table. She did not believe in fate, or predestination, but was willing to recognise serendipity wherever it arose. And for whatever reason, it had risen yesterday, cementing her shaky ideas of rebellion. When Captain Nex had ordered Azrael relocated to level nine, in order to keep level eleven clear and ready for the Final Meld, the chances of spiriting Azrael out of the Facility rose. All eyes were on the Four, and level eleven. Tamas had barely acknowledged the Captain's request for the transfer. A nod, a muttered approval, and the conversation was concluded. Since declaring the Final Meld, Tamas's demeanour had changed. Grown so distracted he looked straight through her. Though they had required her assistance in the tech rooms for some minor issues last night, Blake's time in the inner circle appeared to have come to an abrupt halt. Any other time the sudden invisibility would have riled her.

'Blake?' Rossiter's bulky shadow fell across her keyboard.

'I need you to view something that's occurred at the Wheel and Barrow.' Blake gestured to the recorded footage. Perry on his knees, back arched at an unnatural angle. Despite having watched it several times, it still roiled her stomach.

She hit the playback button, and the video recommenced. Perry's mouth widened, but no sound escaped him. His body jerked and twisted in all manner of unnatural angles, head flicking back and forth like a deranged dancer.

'Jesus,' Rossiter hissed. 'What is happening to him? Is it a seizure?'

Blake's least-favoured words fell bitterly from her lips. 'I do not know.'

Her lack of understanding drove her to distraction. To be at the heart of things and yet still know so little was torturous.

The dark hue of Perry's face deepened further. Suffocation, or choking, Blake decided on her third viewing.

'Did you call an ambulance?' Rossiter dug his broad hand into his pant pocket, but Blake shook her head. Just that slight movement dizzied her. An occurrence growing more frequent as Cym's latest potion lost its lustre.

'No. I was asleep when this occurred. Keep watching.'

Perry jumped to his feet, jerking upright as if invisible strings hauled him upward. The image wavered, and static lines criss-crossed the screen. Though Perry stood, his own legs did not seem to support him. His knees bent, threatening to buckle altogether, but he somehow remained upright. He spun towards the camera. For one brief second his eyes fixed on the lens, and in the black-and-white image, they glinted as an animal's would when caught in a car's headlights. Except there were no headlights, no lights at all in the corner where the camera watched over the bar. The only lights on in the place were the soft overheads above the dark wood of the bar.

Then the spark disappeared. And Perry collapsed, lying with arms and legs splayed. The very position he remained in now, on the live feed. Blake turned to Rossiter, and her self-doubt immediately faded. This was no visual hallucination. No overreaction on her part. And a wrenching disappointment gripped her.

'Christ, Blake.' Rossiter squinted, leaning in close to the screen. 'What just happened to him?'

She refused to admit lack of understanding yet again. 'You saw it too? The odd light at the end? The interference with the TV circuit?'

'I saw a man who needs medical care. That is Kira's closest friend; we need to at least call an ambulance. But I don't understand, why are you watching the Wheel and Barrow?'

Habit, and gut instinct, had seen her call on Rossiter. With the weakening of her body had come a clouding of her mind. And had, if the hallucinations she'd been experiencing were to be believed, begun to affect her senses. She did not have a ginger cat in her townhouse. Nor was it possible that her father had called out to her from the empty kitchen. Yet she had seen and heard both. She needed to be absolutely certain what was on the screen was real.

'I believe this may have something to do with Azrael.'

Rossiter frowned. 'What are you talking about?' His voice dipped to a strained growl. 'Tell me Kira is still in her townhouse.'

'No. She is not.'

'Bloody hell.' He swept his hand over his bald head, a habitual movement related to his stress levels. 'That stupid girl, did she not learn the first time?'

Now was the moment Blake should interject. Defend her sister's actions and admit her involvement in all this. Blake ran unsteady fingers over the fading groove in her cheek. 'We both know that Kira is not a ready learner. Her dependence on alcohol continues to cloud her faculties. I should have been more vigilant. Despite my instruction, she has taken Azrael off Facility grounds. A short time after she and Azrael left the pub, this occurred. I don't believe Azrael was involved directly, but I do believe something preternatural has occurred.'

A reputation was a more powerful tool than the truth in this instance. The longer Blake concealed her involvement, the more readily she could lead those who searched for the gallu down a false trail. Granted, Rossiter's loyalty was undoubted, but he wasn't the one she distrusted. It was the means by which the Syranians and Tamas might attempt to withdraw information from him regarding Azrael's whereabouts. Rossiter's physical strength was impressive, but they would not simply beat information out of him. And Blake would not give up her prize. The tangible link to further understanding. It had been a gamble extricating Azrael, but it had already brought a pay-off. As undesirable as Perry's state may be, it was proof that the Syranians' purpose here was far more nefarious than ever declared, than she had ever allowed herself to believe. The Four hunted for one man, so they said. Well, a man was already dead and the four carapaces were still unfilled.

'Kira is out of control. I told you a long time ago the girl needed to be put into rehab.' Disapproval fell hard and sharp. Rossiter had been a longtime friend of her father's and shared his inability to conceal emotions. Positive or otherwise.

'And you were right. But this is hardly the moment to discuss my sister's shortcomings.'

'Do the Syranians know of Azrael's absence? I haven't heard any alarms being raised.'

'No. They are unaware.' Blake rose to her feet and braced against the table as the room spun. 'And I wish to keep it that way for now. They are preoccupied. I believe there is still time to return Azrael before they are even unaware he is missing. I want you to go to the pub and retrieve Perry. If he lives…' Her voice caught on the words, and she cleared her throat. 'If he lives, there is a rural hospital where I have a contact. I can make it worth their while to treat him with the utmost discretion. The hospital is desperate for new equipment, I understand.'

'Blake, do you think Perry is still alive?'

'It seems unlikely.' She swallowed against a parched throat. In an ironic twist, the Waters plagued her with a dreadful thirst on occasion. She strode to the bottom of the stairs, pausing there, contemplating her chances of walking to the top without displaying obvious signs of fatigue.

'This will destroy her.' Rossiter's deep voice seemed to fill the space.

Blake frowned. 'Who?'

'Your sister, Blake. Kira. I think Perry is the only true

damn friend she's got. And this is her fault. Her stupid mistake.' He lowered his eyes, and his next word was barely audible. 'Again.'

The handrail bit into Blake's thigh, her full body weight against it. All the heat drained from her and she shivered. 'Nothing can be done about that right now. Please go. Take one of the helicopters. Get to Perry before anyone else does.'

Rossiter strode past her on the steps without another word. Leaving her alone in the basement. When he reached the front door upstairs, he slammed it hard enough to rattle the windows.

Blake made her cautious way to the top of the stairs, taking it slow across the kitchen, into the hall and up another flight of stairs to her bedroom. Vertigo plagued her every step of the way. And just when she thought herself safe, seated on the edge of her bed the contents of her stomach pushed up against the back of her throat. Zigzagging, she made it to the bathroom but failed to reach the toilet. The floor and her clothing suffered for it.

Twenty minutes later she headed back downstairs, snail's pace, skin damp from her shower, face reddened by the heat of the water. The mauve linen shirt she'd pulled on needed laundering, but it was closest to hand and she didn't have the energy to give a damn. Her black linen pants were awash with creases and hung around her hips.

Reaching the lounge room, her attention went straight to her mobile phone resting on the coffee table. No flashes of light to indicate the bodyguard had anything important to relay. She was far too eager. Chances were he'd only just lifted off. The doorbell announced a visitor and Blake jumped. She made her way to the front door, pulse racing at a ludicrous speed. Rossiter would not use the bell. She jabbed at the monitor by the side of the door, and a little of the panic subsided.

Blake pulled the door open.

'Cym, how can I help you?'

The tall Syranian nodded in greeting. High cheekbones shadowed by the porch light. 'Blake, I thought I might have a moment of your time. There is something I'd like to discuss . . .' His shaped, dark eyebrows furrowed. 'You have been unwell?'

A blush warmed her cheeks. The Syranians' sense of smell was remarkable, and humiliating. 'No more than usual.'

Fatigue and anxiety gave her words a harshness Cym did not deserve. She had worked closely with the Syranians from the day of their extraterrestrial arrival. Though he was a medic essentially, his limited knowledge of engineering had proved far more important when only a fraction of the Syranian fleet had survived the journey to Earth. As Blake assumed her place as Technician, in the absence of those sent for the task, Cym had been at her side. And he'd not hesitated to conceal her declining health from those, namely the captain, who would view it less favourably and see it as an opportunity to remove 'human interference' altogether.

'I'm sorry, please, come in.'

She stepped aside, and he entered the room. His movement always reminded her of the loping gait of a giraffe. Clumsy and yet impossibly elegant at the same time.

'I have been developing the treatment for you.' Brown contact lenses hid his white eyes, giving his gaze a warmth that was absent in reality. 'The last dosage was promising. This I believe, may bring further relief. I must warn you, there could be side effects –'

'I don't care.' Blake held out her hand. 'I'm assuming you have them with you, hence the visit.'

His narrow lips curved with a smile. The Syranians had adopted the habit since their arrival, and Cym was by far the most adept at it. 'Correct. And I'll admit it seems odd to not have been with you for almost a day, after working so closely for so long.'

He moved close and cupped her hand with his own, dwarfing hers, then placed a small velvet pouch in her open palm. 'Intravenous, I'm afraid. But with your stomach already experiencing duress, this mixture may prove too harsh in tablet form.'

'I'm fine with needles.'

Cym withdrew his grip, but her assurance was contradicted by the shaking of her hand.

'Allow me, Blake.'

She didn't protest as he withdrew the vial and narrow syringe from the pouch. They seated themselves on the couch, and she watched his narrow fingers work to fill the syringe with grey-tinted fluid.

'We will commence with a very limited dose. Ascertain side effects.' Cym pressed the needle to the crux of her arm, her veins blue-green against her pale skin. Blake bit down on her lip. 'I apologise.'

She shook her head. 'No need. It's fine. I'm fine.' A pinch, a sting, nothing horrendous, but uncomfortable all the same.

Brown eyes lifted and fixed on her. 'Of course.'

The fluid made its way through her system, warm and unexpectedly soothing. The sigh escaped her before she could stop it. Cym withdrew the needle, heading into the kitchen to dispose of it. She realised that, aside from Rossiter, Cym was likely the only other visitor who had crossed her threshold in months. The Syranian displayed a curiosity about human invention and ingenuity that was impossible to dismiss. He wondered over the simplest things: toasters, microwaves. Electric toothbrushes. Around him, Blake enjoyed some taste of what it must feel like to be the advanced race.

The shaking in her hands lessened, not disappearing entirely but becoming far easier to conceal. Knots she didn't realise she held began to unwind. In her belly, her shoulders. Blake relaxed against the leather couch, sinking into its softness. She must have dozed off, because when the banging at the door commenced, the shock of the sound almost caused her to lurch from the seat. Cym rose from the armchair to her left with all his usual grace and calm.

'Who is that?' Blake demanded, rising to her feet. She noted with relief that the world did not spin.

'I have no idea.' Cym frowned. 'I remained to ensure nothing untoward happened. You have been sleeping, and I was about to return to prepare for Service.'

Blake glanced at her watch. Five-thirty in the morning. She'd lost an hour and a half. With no call from Rossiter. The tension began to curl back into her tired muscles.

The person demanding entry hammered at the front door. 'Blake, open up, or I'll open it up for you.'

Blake crossed the lounge room, walking in a straight line, her breath coming easily. Short-term at least, Cym's treatment was working. She swung the door open, coming face to face with Nari and Reuben, Tamas's shadows.

'You need to come with me, Blake. The boss has a few questions for you.' Nari's hand hung casually, but pointedly, by her sidearm. She glanced over Blake's shoulder. 'Well, I didn't realise the exotic taste extended to you too, Blake. Good morning, Cym.'

'Nari,' came the stilted reply.

'Tamas has questions about what, Nari?' Blake tucked her trembling hands into her pant pockets, remaining outwardly calm.

Reuben spoke up, his blank expression betraying little. 'About what you have done with Azrael.'

'What are you talking about? The gallu is contained underground.'

'You already know that is not the case.' Blake's heart raced with sudden, violent palpitations. Reuben stared at her like she'd grown a secondary head, while Nari's lips pressed with a disapproving frown.

'Miss Beckworth?' Reuben took a step towards her.

It would have been an ideal way to ensure questioning of any sort was delayed, faking a sudden illness. But there was nothing fake about her display. Blake opened her mouth to reply, but her crazed pulse filled every vein to bursting. Her throat tightened, contracted in on itself. As did her vision. Until all that remained was a fuzzy image of three faces huddled over her.

ERON - 13

Eron's tongue curved through the holy words of service. His voice dipped low with the guttural sounds of the homage to Lahar. There had been no slumber for him the evening before, after the captain advised Eron he would be allowed to attend this morning's service. Bel led the prayers, kneeling beneath the Precon beast carved into the ceiling of Lahar's Shrine. His usual passion was amplified on this morning. Gren, to his right, was equally vocal, his thin voice echoing Bel's enthusiasm. Seder and Parator knelt just in front of Eron. Their adorations were less vociferous, but their faces held an uncharacteristic brightness.

Eron was not deemed worthy to enter the circle formed around the petrified trunk at the heart of the shrine, and so crouched behind his brothers. But the continued slight did not dampen his fervour this morning. He was in attendance on this momentous day. It was enough.

Eron lifted his head. The goddess's totem was carved into the far wall in such a way that the wolf's enormous eyes followed wherever one might stand in the shrine. The glass creature's stare did not suggest the goddess wished to disembowel him, as it had a week ago when he'd fallen asleep beneath her.

Much had changed this week. Azrael's successful Meld had lifted spirits. The approach of their end goal after so much time spent waiting had buoyed Captain Nex into gracing Eron with a brief, but very discernible, nod when they passed in the halls now. And of far greater significance, the captain had ordered Eron's immediate inclusion in group training sessions with Azrael and the mea stones. Not that he'd been fully excluded to begin with. With only seven Syranians surviving the journey across the vastness of space, there had been little chance Eron would be totally ostracised, no matter what he'd done with a human woman. But until now he'd endured training with the captain alone. And Captain Nex was consistently in a foul and demanding mood. Eron's technique, his level of telekinetic control over the gallu, was never satisfactory.

Eron shifted, trying to ease the pinch of the hard surface against his knees. Right at that exact moment, the singing ceased and the group fell into reflective silence. He recoiled at the coarse sound his pants made against the smooth glass. Seder threw a sharp sideways glance, his thin lips curling with displeasure. Eron dipped his head in supplication, but even Seder's sourness could not disturb him.

It was a momentous day. Which made Captain Nex's absence all the more disquieting.

Gren tilted his head, catching Eron's eye and mouthing something at him.

The captain? Gren shrugged his narrow but muscled shoulders, strands of his loosened black hair shifting with the movement.

Eron shrugged in return. *Cym?*

Gren shook his head and returned to silent prayer, confusion edging thin lines into his smooth dark skin.

Cym's absence might be accounted for, with the preparations of the carapaces, but the captain's was far more curious. Though, truthfully, Eron did not find himself entirely disappointed. He returned his concentration to the floor, where the emerald Waters streamed beneath them.

In this very shrine, two days past, the goddess's Messenger, the stuttering and awkward human Tamas, had received the Word they'd waited on. Azrael had proved the stability of the carapaces and the ability of the artificial shells to sustain the gallu on Earth. At Azrael's expense, the Syranians had mastered the mea stones – the reins, as it were, that would enable them to control the immensely powerful gallu soon to arrive.

Today, these divine hunters would step foot again in this world. Absent for millennia, the Four would search for Dumuzi, the immortal soul bound inside a fragile human shell.

Eron stared into the shadows dancing within the light in the Waters. He liked to imagine what appearance Dumuzi's mortal shell might take. Robust, or frail? Indeed, male or female? What did a demigod wrapped in a human look like? Dumuzi was the last remnant of a different time here on Earth. The demigod husband of a great goddess who had long since departed these corporeal worlds, abandoning her lover to a fate that should have been hers. Inanna and Ereshkigal might be divine sisters, but their relationship was as fraught with difficulty as the one that existed between Kira and Blake Beckworth. Mere mortals.

Eron closed his eyes, attempting to shut out the image of Kira that rose. He pressed his fingertips to the glass, focusing on the energy emanating there. Perhaps it was ludicrous to compare the humans to the goddesses. An argument between Kira and Blake did not threaten worlds, or universes. Their contempt for one another did not continue unabated for time immemorial. It did not drive them to grasp at any opportunity, however miniscule, to humiliate and hinder the other, as it did for Ereshkigal and Inanna. But what fuelled the ferocity of the relationship was not so different. Blood.

A connection that could not be undone. Whatever might be the desire.

But where grief fed the flames between Kira and Blake, it was a lust for power that burned between Ereshkigal and Inanna.

After Inanna's failed attempt to take her sister's throne and rule the underworld, Ereshkigal had imprisoned Inanna's divine soul in the pathetic shroud of a human body and sentenced her to an eternity on Earth. But Inanna was not so unlike Kira.

Eron smothered a wry smile. Inanna was a master manipulator and wily negotiator. When Ereshkigal sent the Four to imprison her, Innana offered up her husband Dumuzi's soul instead and fled the corporeal worlds for the next realm. But grudges between the deities lasted eternally. And so, here Eron knelt, thrust into the ongoing conflict by the will of his god Lahar. One of the last Living Gods – a meagre group of three – who battled to ascend from the mortal worlds to the next realm. Lahar had chosen a side, hoping to be granted favour by a far more powerful god of the realm. He'd allied himself with Ereshkigal, providing the Waters, the Syranian god-soldiers, and the mea stones, all required to enable the Four to find the human shell holding Dumuzi and destroy the demigod's soul. If so done, Inanna would be forced to take Dumuzi's place.

Rules were rules, no matter how ancient or rusty they had become. Innana would be forced into a human prison.

The goddess of war, locked in a foreign, unwanted body.

No. Kira was not so different to Inanna in many ways. Eron leaned his full weight upon his fingertips, and the minute muscles within his fingers protested. Who knew what would remain of this world with Inanna imprisoned within? Subtle coils of guilt rose, cool and unpleasant, through Eron's core, as they often did when considering the strife he and his Lord brought with their mission. He rubbed at the mea stone embedded in his forearm, a sudden ache pulsing through the muscles surrounding it.

The stone's hue resembled that of the desert surrounding them. Its rough edges were now buried beneath his own flesh. A week before he'd left Syrana, it had been embedded just below the prominent veins in Eron's wrist, deep enough to attach to bone. The woman who had conducted the procedure was likely deceased now. Eron's parents would have passed long before her. It had taken twenty-seven Earth years to propel them from Syrana to the blue planet. Most of those years had been spent in the unmemorable blackness of stasis, and as Eron and his brethren had glided through the emptiness of space, sixty years had passed by on Syrana. Time widened the gap between Eron and home until it was stretched beyond all repair. His life there, the people he cared for, all now gone.

'Eron.' The whisper, so close by, caused him to start. Parator stood at his side, glaring in the baleful way he was so adept at. 'Service has been suspended. Rise.'

Eron did so at the expense of grace, his haste rocking him on his feet in much the way it had after several glasses of what Kira referred to as 'cat's piss'. The captain hastened across the greater Orientation Room at a quick pace. Bel moved down the short flight of steps out of the shrine to meet their leader, the others close behind.

'Captain.' Bel pressed a balled fist to his left shoulder and bowed low enough to ensure that his head dipped below the captain's heart line, as was protocol. Not a difficult task for Bel, considering his relatively short stature. For Eron, being taller than his captain, it was a more dramatic gesture. Eron bowed, stomach muscles engaging with the low tilt of his body.

'Rise.' Captain Nex always held a suggestion of robustness and coiled intensity. He was narrow of face and sharp of facial structure, and his nose and chin were equal in their cuspidate definition. The captain's eyes were set beneath thick dark eyebrows, while silver-white hair hung in two bound separations framing his face, their lengths reaching midchest. 'Pigtails', Kira called the style. Something she found amusing for reasons Eron had never understood. Warmth filled his face. Truly he must be mad. To think of her in this moment.

'There is an issue. One that requires a quick resolution.' Captain Nex was not a demonstrative communicator. It was rare, if not impossible, to glean any sense of context through his tone, delivering good and bad news alike in an impassive way. 'We have received word that the gallu . . . Azrael . . . has been removed from the Facility by the Lesser.'

Eron kept his gaze indirect, an expected protocol for anyone being addressed by the captain, but his thoughts were calamitous. Nex referred to Kira as the Lesser of the two sisters, ever begrudging the resources used to save the girl's life.

'How is that possible?' Gren said.

Eron felt the pressure of his brothers' gazes upon him, Seder's the most pointed of all. Eron pulled back his shoulders, refusing to meet their accusatory stares. Aside from the brief encounter on level eleven a week ago, he'd not been in Kira's company. And by the grace of Lahar, that encounter remained unknown to his brethren. He had no clue how Kira had actually removed Azrael, but if it had been similar to his own breach, she had simply driven him out the front gates. Her Telteriun body parts distracted the Lucentshield from the gallu's energy signature, the same way they'd concealed that of his mea stone.

The captain's eyes fixed on him with an intensity that could crack glass. Eron lowered his head.

'Yet again I find myself regretting the day the Lesser was allowed to live,' Nex growled. 'But we have located the vehicle they are traveling in.' The captain stopped in front of Eron. Heavy black boots, polished to perfection, reflected the emerald Waters. 'You are to take assistance and retrieve Azrael.'

Eron continued to stare at his leader's boots, fervently hoping it was not Seder who had received the order. His sullen-faced brother would not make things pleasant for Kira. So far as Seder was concerned, god-soldiers did not soil themselves with something as base as physical contact with humans. His disgust at Eron's indiscretion ran deep, likely because Seder's own irascible temperament rendered him so intensely unattractive. To any living being.

'Eron.'

Eron jerked upright, a flush of heat filling his body. 'Sir? I am to retrieve the gallu?' He stuttered over the words, and the captain's eyes narrowed.

'It is our lord's will.' And Captain Nex sounded none too pleased about it. 'Lahar bids me to send you.' He tilted his head towards the shrine. Eron turned to find the Precon beast, Lahar's totem, had shifted from its place inside the structure. Now the fanged and clawed creature's image was cut into the glass wall nearest to Eron. One huge paw lifted, as though reaching for him. Eron fell to his knees, crossing his arms across his chest in supplication. A thrill rang through his body; nerve endings buzzed.

'Lord Lahar, your spirit be ever uplifted.' Eron touched his forehead to the coolness of the concrete. 'I do your bidding. Evermore. Thank you for your generosity. Your forgiveness.'

By the time he'd settled back onto his haunches, the Precon glass etching had disappeared, returning to its place alongside Ereshkigal's wolf inside the shrine. The wall in front of Eron was smooth again.

'Do not disappoint, Eron. Lahar has given you an opportunity to redeem yourself and show your true commitment to our task. But do not overassume your importance. Your god-soldier brothers cannot be expended; their time to Bind with the Four fast approaches, and they cannot be sent on trivial missions such as this. A Syranian must be in attendance should the gallu attempt to protest recapture, and you are the only one I can spare. Return the gallu to his rightful place, and bring in the Lesser so that we might punish her, as she should have been punished before now.'

Eron fought to keep his expression neutral. The captain was Lahar's Messenger, but Eron sensed this directive had not come from the god himself at all. Despite the spectacle of the Precon beast's movement within the shrine, he suspected Lahar was busy with far greater complications than a once-disobedient god-soldier and a human girl who strove to drive people to distraction.

This was the captain's own test. An offered opportunity for Eron to redeem himself fully in the eyes of his brethren. And, dare he imagine it, an opportunity to Bind with one of the Four?

'Sir.' Eron nodded. 'Be assured, I will not fail. I will leave immediately.'

Twenty minutes later, eyes stinging and itchy with the contact lenses he wore, Eron was strapped into the helicopter and on his way to Lorhurst, the town Kira's vehicle had been tracked to. The first time aboveground in several months and it was difficult to keep the smile from his face. He pushed down the access window, letting the warm air blast his face, taking long, slow breaths of it. He relished the different scents upon the breeze. Seated at the back of the craft, behind the accompanying guards – two women and a man – Eron tugged his hair from its bind, and it tumbled down around his face. The strands whipped chaotically as the helicopter lifted off. Bliss.

It was early morning, barely after eight, and the desert beneath them was already fully lit by the glowing morning sun. Eron craned his neck to take in everything that passed below them. The signs of life that had been closed off to him for many long months. Lorhurst. Something about the name niggled at him. The helicopter skirted around Pryden and headed east.

'Sir,' the pilot interrupted Eron's attempt to source his unease, 'I'm getting information that there's been an incident in Pryden. At the Wheel and Barrow.' He hesitated. 'Kira Beckworth owns the –'

'I'm aware.' Eron pressed the mouthpiece closer. 'What is the issue?'

'Patching you through to a secure frequency. Stand by.'

A click, a hum, and then a new and unfamiliar voice. 'Sir, information relay. Dwayne Rossiter was intercepted at the Wheel and Barrow while attempting to extract a man who has sustained significant life-threatening injuries. You are advised that evidence suggests utukku are involved. You are to be aware of the increased presence of supermundanes. End secure transmission.'

Another click, two this time, and a high-pitched buzz as the radio reconnected him with the pilot.

'Sir, advising we will reach destination in ten minutes.'

'Very good,' Eron said absently.

Supermundanes were commonplace on Syrana due to Lahar's divine presence. Utukku, possession spirits, certainly caused issues every now and then. But this was Earth, a world devoid of its deities for thousands of years. The preternatural survivors here would have been in hibernation all that time and weakened to the very edge of existence. Certainly, with the arrival of the Waters, and the Four, on Earth, it was expected that any entities that had survived in this godless world might stir. But for an uttuku to be strong enough already to cause near-fatal injuries was perplexing. Azrael was no god. It could not be his presence alone that had fuelled such a rise.

The helicopter descended, and as Eron stared down at the layout of the small town, the niggle returned. A sense of familiarity gripped him at the sight of the clock tower at the town's heart. The pilot lowered them a mile from the tower in an industrial area. Touching down, the others waited for Eron's directive, placing themselves at a discreet distance, using protocol, he suspected, as an excuse to keep from his immediate vicinity.

He stood in the middle of the road, a patchwork of

asphalt and faded line markings. The disused lot they had landed in was one of several on this stretch of road, peppered with old warehouses that clearly had not been frequented in some time, weeds growing high in cracks in the parking lots, and unrepaired holes dotting roofs.

Now he understood what it was that had disquieted him. He had been to this place. Lorhurst. With Kira. She had declared it a shithole, and they had driven through it at a speed that had alarmed him, heading for somewhere brighter and bigger. Full of those crowded, loud places she loved to frequent.

'Bore-hurst'. Was the name Kira had bestowed on this town. Refusing to stop even when he professed a desire to view the clock tower more closely.

'Sir, the vehicle is just over there.' A guard pointed to a great pile of old tyres.

But Eron did not move.

Kira was not here. She had never been here. The Lesser had played her denigrators as masterfully as the goddess Inanna herself. And Eron could not suppress the smile that rose to his lips.

KIRA - 14

Wheels hit runway just after eight in the morning. The bumpy landing jerked Kira awake. Bankston Regional Airport, a glorious stark-white tin shed in the middle of a field. Kira stepped out of the aircraft.

'Doesn't get more glam than this.' She stretched her arms over her head, the armadillo hidden beneath the dreaded sheath, and waited till Az joined her before she headed down the stairs. She was bleary-eyed, and definitely had bad breath but surprisingly chipper despite the number of whiskies consumed. There was an advantage to buying the good stuff to knock yourself unconscious. She wore a baseball cap, a pair of rose-gold-coloured shades that probably cost as much as a small country, and a bob-cut blonde wig.

Blake had gone full super spy. And it was kind of awesome. Though it would have been nice if she'd also packed a toothbrush and deodorant, clean knickers. Instead it was a disguise and cash. Lots and lots of green notes. Kira herded a docile Azrael into a taxi and threw the duffel bag in alongside him. Their driver looked as though he wanted to kiss her when Kira asked for the ride. Business was slow apparently. He was old enough to be her grandfather, wore the proverbial Coke-bottle glasses, and clearly had no clue who she was, so he was perfect. They were invisible.

She gave him directions to Melgrove, but had no intention of reaching the place. There were a couple of smaller, even lamer towns before it that would do nicely. Fifteen minutes later she got the driver to pull over in a place called Shallow River, made all the more amusing by the utterly dry riverbed circling the town. Then into another taxi and heading south, where she repeated the exercise once more. Blake wasn't the only one who'd watched a Bond movie or two. Good luck to anyone trying to trace them.

She hit pay dirt in a town called Eaglemont, where she homed in on a taxi driver who sported a thick silver wedding ring and a pair of eyes that kept dropping to her chest. Her waist. Anywhere but her eyes. This would do nicely. She shoved Az into the back seat and went up front with the driver.

'Beleiro, thanks.' Kira settled into her seat, arching her back with a slow languid sigh. 'It's been a long day.' She swept her hands over her chest and down to the waist of her pants. Roving Eyes followed every move. Lips lifting in a not-unattractive smile. Kira smiled back, letting her eyes dip to his crotch ever so briefly. A chew on her bottom lip, a coy tilt of her head.

'Are you a dancer?' he asked.

He needed a shave, but if this had to go further, Kira would manage. The guy had some impressive bulges. Pecs trying to bust his shirt sleeves. Too much product in his wavy brown hair, one too many chains around his neck. This guy wanted a whole lot more than driving a cab in the middle of butt-fuck nowhere. She'd met his doppelgänger more than a few times.

She giggled. It had been a long time between these sorts of giggles, but the best way to stay invisible was to fuck around with a married man. Guilt was a great gag. 'No. I'm an entertainer, though.'

'Got it. Used to do a bit of entertaining myself, back in the day. Your boyfriend?' He jerked his head towards Az.

Kira shook her head in a slow back-and-forth. 'Just a friend. He doesn't like what I've got.'

Queue more smiles, another dose of giggles, inane chatting while fucking the guy with her eyes. Twenty minutes later, they hit the outskirts of Beleiro. The casino town was still half-asleep at this hour. Traffic minimal. The cabbie's hand rested on her thigh; her legs parted just enough to let his fingers slide a little lower.

'Turn off up here, on the right.' Kira laid her hand over his. 'I'm working in there.' She nodded towards the pyramid-shaped building they were passing. Shit of a place. Beds like planks. Definitely not where they would be staying, but Roving Eyes didn't need to know that. 'Az, get out of the car. Just need to pay our lovely driver here. I'll be five minutes.'

It took two. The guy's fuse was on the short side, and the dynamite was loaded and ready to go. Fare paid, Kira jumped out of the cab, wiping her hand against her pant leg. The car pulled away, and the driver didn't look back – too busy cleaning his ring – leaving them in an alleyway that stank of piss.

'And that is the holy trinity right there, my friend. Prostitution, adultery, and tax evasion. That dick just made us totally invisible.' Kira raised her clenched fist. 'Fist bump. Hit me.'

Az stared at her. Arms by his side.

'Rather I washed my hands first? Don't blame you.' Kira gave him a wry smile and slung the duffel bag over her shoulder. 'Come on, we're –'

'Hit me,' Az said. Coughed, really.

'Jesus. You talk now? Do it again.'

But Az seemed to have spooked himself. He touched his fingers to the soft skin around his pink lips. Sucking at the air, then pressing his mouth closed, too tight, as if he were trying to push out a giant fart. Open again. Closed again.

'Okay, don't do that,' Kira said. 'Not a good look.'

'Good look,' Azrael said. His fingers dropped to his throat, as though the sound startled him. It wasn't an especially notable sound: not too deep, not too high. Just a male voice.

'Okay, so you can mimic,' she said. 'Awesome. I'm on the run with a parrot.'

'Parrot,' Azrael said. He might have been smiling, or it was gas again. Hard to tell.

'Hilarious.' Kira raised her metal arm, hidden in its faux skin, aiming to give him a playful thump on the shoulder. He flinched. Hard.

'My bad.' Kira lowered her arm. 'It's okay. It's okay. Look, see it doesn't hurt.'

She punched her thigh, punching too hard in her enthusiasm to show how nonthreatening she was. It hurt like hell.

'Whatever, let's just get inside. I'm sweating like a fucking pig.'

The sun was well and truly up, the sky a stunning

turquoise blue, completely clear. They headed away from the pyramid building, walking two blocks before she chose the Aldrovandi. Gaudy faux Italian Renaissance architecture, gardens manicured to within an inch of their lives. She'd been to Beleiro a couple of times but never stayed there.

'Now, you need to keep quiet, okay? You're a very hot parrot, but Parrot needs to be super quiet for now.'

She glanced at the tranq bracelet. It was down as low as the bloody thing would allow without flashing its brains out at her, but maybe it should be up a little. Dope him out. Just for the foray to their room. Kira eased the level up a couple of notches.

'Sorry, dude. This won't be for long.'

When Az had been staring at a ripped poster on a lamppost for several minutes, Kira took him by the elbow and guided him up the sweeping circular drive of the Aldrovandi.

They got all the way through the enormous gilded front doors, across the ridiculously spacious, might-be-real-marble foyer, and up to the reception desk. No real issues, save for a few looks. Azrael didn't say a word, wide-eyed at the world around him like a kid in a candy store.

Deluxe suite booked for two nights. If on the run, do it in style. Handing over cash here was no big deal, and the girl at the reception desk barely looked at Kira's ID, the one that said she was a blonde Clara Oswald and thirty-two years old. Mildly insulting that the woman didn't challenge the age. If she pulled her eyes away from Azrael for one second, the check-in chick would totally realise Kira was so much younger. The brunette with the rosy cheeks giggled way too much, and either her lips needed some lip balm, or the lip-licking was an attempt to be seductive. Poor bitch. What a waste of time. Az blinked at her, did a few little fish pouts with his lips. Fuck's sake, that move had to go.

'We're going to need a champagne breakfast as soon as you can deliver it,' Kira said.

'Certainly. I'll arrange that now. Here are your key cards.' The woman handed them to Azrael. He stared at them.

'Thanks.' Kira grabbed the cards. 'How quick can you get the champagne breakfast up there?'

'I'll have it sent right away, madam.' She gave Kira a nod, but her eyes snaked back to Azrael.

'Great. Less eggs more champagne, thanks.'

The woman gave her another absent nod. Kira declined an offer to have luggage taken to their room, then herded Az into a half-full elevator, shuffling past a young family with a toddler who wasn't going to give up trying to press all the buttons. The only other occupants were a couple who Kira was pretty sure hadn't been to bed yet. Judging by the way the guys kept touching each other, there was no sleep on the horizon, either. It was only when Kira saw one of them, a portly suited gentleman with stunningly white teeth, giving Azrael a bemused look that she realised what Az was doing. Nothing. He stood facing the back of the elevator, inches away from the mirrored wall. Kira gave the portly guy a smile she hoped said, *He's wasted*, and then tried to get Az to turn around. Which was not going to happen. He was giving the mirror a stare that could bore holes in it.

Kira gave up. Weird shit happened in this town; a narcissist wouldn't cause a raised eyebrow. The elevator doors closed, cringe-worthy music started, and up they went.

'Can you press level twenty-five, please?' she said.

'Oh, nice floor.' The portly man's partner – also suited but more bookish, less Wall Street – gave her a wink and tapped the twenty-five. 'We were up there last year for our honeymoon. I'm not worth it this year, apparently.'

The portly man gave him an indulgent smile and a light tap on the backside, then nodded to Azrael.

'Is he okay?'

'Oh yeah,' Kira said. 'Fine. Jetlag and a couple of early gins. You know how it is.'

The guys laughed that too-hard way people do when they are drunk. Kira tried again to shift Azrael, but he was boulder heavy. He leaned in closer to the mirror and pressed his fingers against his reflection. The guy didn't know what a napkin was for, no surprise his reflection had him stumped, but it was going to be awkward if they got to their level and he wouldn't leave the elevator. At least he wasn't parroting everyone. The elevator stopped, and the young family got out. The little girl waved to everyone as her father tried to pull her out of the elevator.

'Goodbye.'

Kira didn't find miniature humans appealing in any shape or form, but it caught Azrael's attention. He lifted his hand and mimicked her wave with a much slower one of his own. Only, he wasn't looking at the little girl. He was looking at himself.

'Goodbye,' he said, barely above a whisper. 'Goodbye.'

He pressed his head against the glass and made another sound, a hell of a lot like a sob. The elevator was getting way too small. The guys got off two floors later, and she assured them she didn't need any help with Az. He'd be just fine. They told her their room number, and the bookish one blew her a kiss, then Kira and Az were alone. In the end she had no trouble getting him out of the elevator. He turned from his reflection of his own accord. Kept his head down and eyes on the ground all the way up the hall and in through the double door of their suite.

'What's going on, Az? You doing okay?' She ran her fingers over the tranq band, pushing the levels down, but the little mechanical bastard wasn't having it and beeped at her. 'Do as you're told, asshat.'

Az was too spacey, even more of an airhead. And that sob. What the fuck was that about? She needed to let him think straight for a moment. Kira manoeuvred him down onto the white leather couch forming an L-shape in the enormous lounge room. The widescreen TV on the wall was enormous, too. Practically a mini cinema screen. Kira pulled off the wig, scratching hard at her scalp. Az sat on the edge of the couch, eyes unfocused, a mute zombie. Blake got that look sometimes. A lot of times, actually. Kira tilted her wrist, considering the matte silver bracelet. Maybe Blake was getting off with these things. Had to be something up with her. Blake Beckworth didn't usually give her little sister multimillion dollar toys to play with.

'Okay, Az. Wakey wakey time. Come on.' Kira flicked on the TV, and it sprang to life on a cooking show. Roast lamb. 'Az, look. Look at this. Yum. Roast lamb.'

Jesus, she sounded like a moron. And being vegetarian, it made her want to puke. Az didn't show any appreciation for her sacrifice. He just stared at the screen. She'd seen vacant expressions before, plenty of them in the clubs, but this was over and above. He wasn't just vacant. He wasn't there.

Kira knelt on the floor in front of him. The pale mauve rug beneath her was sublimely soft and shaggy. Probably had had more naked bodies rolling on it than the bed. Oh god, what she wouldn't do to just be mindlessly fucking right now. Blake thought she was a sex addict. Nope. Kira was just addicted to not thinking too hard.

'Right. I'm just going to interrupt your silent party for one, okay.' She reached for him. 'Don't slam me in the face or anything.'

She waited a second for a reaction. Nothing. So she laid her metal hand, still clad in its faux skin, over his, bracing for impact.

Less impact, more delicate brush this time, though. A tingle where their bodies touched. Not so bad. She slid her fingers in between his, and a gasp escaped her. Nerve endings alive and humming, her body warming with a disquieting post-orgasm-like float. This was new. And a little bit nice. A smile played at her lips. Jesus, she could get used to this. Bliss without the mess.

She'd barely had a chance to enjoy it, and the bliss fled, leaving a deep, gouging sense of loss in its place. No wait, it was confusion. No, hang on, now it was melancholy. Azrael was riding a super shitty rollercoaster, and he was on the Big Dipper, swan diving into a loneliness that dwarfed anything she'd ever felt. Kira wanted to let go. Hell, she wanted to run. Out the door into the sun. She really, really wanted that champagne part of the champagne breakfast. A bottle or two. Anything to block this out. But then he raised his head. Lifted up those drown-me-now green eyes. His hands slid over hers. The shift was subtle at first; the need to cry for a hundred years lingered, but the confusion lessened, unclogging itself from the part of her brain this whole thing was fucking with.

Kira didn't move. They sat there, her knees aching, her throat tense with unshed tears. The room around her blurred, pretty colours bulging and contracting, catching her in a life-size kaleidoscope. She held on. Waiting. Sensing Azrael clawing his way back. As though she were some goddamn lighthouse in the darkness. The shadows fell behind, taking the bad stuff with them. And then he broke through, raising himself up out of the stinking, sickening darkness.

He breathed in and spoke softly on the exhale. 'I know nothing. I don't know who I am.'

His own words. Two full sentences. The sound of his voice broke the spell and reminded her she wasn't actually on some weird trip. She was sitting on a purple rug in a hotel room. Body buzzing. And she wasn't sad. For once, *she* wasn't the lonely, sad, and desperate one. And damn it felt good. Good enough to make a promise she had no idea whether she could keep.

'Then we will find out. I will find out,' she said. 'We'll sort this. Blake will tell me – who you are, what you are. I promise you.'

The connection between them was fading, pulling away like the edges of a high. The withdrawal gained speed till it evaporated into nothing more than a sweet heat deep in her belly. But he was okay. He was back.

For now.

A knock at the door. Perfect timing. Like a *The End* to punctuate the whole thing. Kira got to her feet. Holy crap that champers was going to taste good. Her body was light and humming, and she felt like she needed to adjust her clothes before opening the door. A waiter wheeled in the silver cart and laid out the breakfast on the elaborate black resin coffee table. Azrael hunched forward, head in his hands, not once even glancing at the stranger in the room. Kira signed the bill and closed the door.

'Okay, you know what, we need some of this.'

She pulled the Krug out of its ice bucket and uncorked it, sending the cork flying over somewhere near the massive floor-to-ceiling windows that ran the length of the suite. The view took in a football-pitch-size man-made lake. Four elaborate fountains were in the midst of hurling firework-like spurts of water into the air in time with coloured lights and music that barely penetrated the apartment. She handed Azrael a full glass. Whether he could drink or not she didn't give a shit. This called for something. He stared at the glass in her hand before taking the offered one, moving it up close to his face, watching the streams of bubbles move through the caramel-gold liquid.

'To you, zombie boy.' Kira raised her glass. 'To learning to talk. Glasses up.'

She encouraged Azrael with an exaggerated lift of her glass. He followed suit, too fast, and the contents of his glass sloshed out, raining down onto the dead-Muppet rug. Azrael shrank back into the couch. The expression on his face was pathetic. Kira burst out laughing, noticing him flinch but not giving a crap. She downed her glass in two sucking gulps, then refilled both their glasses.

'It's all good. Plenty more where that came from.'

The corners of his lips turned up and parted a little, and he did this squishy thing with his nose. In the end he managed to look more like he smelled a dead skunk, but she got the gist. It was an attempt at a smile.

'We'll work on that,' Kira said. 'But well done.'

'Kira.'

That was it. Just one word, but she nearly lost her mouthful of champers all over the snow-white leather.

'Yes.' Hiccups followed the rapid swallow of bubbles. 'That's me. I'm Kira. That's awesome. Say it again.'

He gave her a look, a furrowed brow that said in clear face-talk, *Don't treat me like a dickhead.* And in that disapproving dip of his eyebrows, there was no more denial. What she thought she'd glimpsed before was now plain as the nose on his perfect face. Inside that suit of impossible abs and behind those eyes to die for, there was something alive. Zombie boy was most definitely not a zombie.

Non-zombie boy tipped the glass to his lips and sucked it back in one go.

Two hours later, and two more bottles of bubbles, the scrambled eggs were cold as ice, but Kira shoved them in her mouth regardless. She was drunk. Not unusual but very unintended. It was just after eleven in the morning, which would normally have been a great time to *start* drinking. Curling up in the enormous king-plus-size bed seemed a much better idea. Two hours of shut-eye on the plane hadn't really cut it.

'Are you feeling anything?' Kira shoved the eggs against her cheek so she could talk. Champagne on an empty stomach was such a bad, bad idea.

'I feel no different.' Azrael refused to let her change the channel from the shopping network. He had a serious thing for special-occasion jewellery. Shiny stuff was giving him a hard-on. Well, not literally. She didn't think. He was sitting on the floor close to the TV, and every time the ads were done he ignored her. She got it. That sparkly shit was so damn pretty, Kira was seriously considering buying a tiara; but what she really wanted was to keep talking. She sat down beside him, plate in hand.

'So the words thing,' Kira said. 'What's with that? Did you like pull the knowledge out of my brain or something? Some kind of synaptic connection that means you know all the words I know. Sorry, dude, you are going to know a lot of really fucked up words.'

She laughed. Azrael did not. A rebellious egg fleck made a break for it down her throat, and Kira's giggle turned into a cough and choke. Azrael's gaze didn't leave the screen.

'I believe I could always speak,' he said. 'The knowledge was mine, not yours.'

'Fine. Then why have you been a boring mute since you . . .' *Since you got here? Since you were born? Since you were made?* She couldn't choose one, so she let it slide.

For the first time in about thirty minutes, he looked away from the TV. She was sitting very close to him; if she were to lean ever so slightly, her knee would touch his leg.

'It was as though the words could not make it to this tongue.' He peered at her as if the answer were in her irises somewhere. 'I don't understand. I do not know why it was difficult, only that it is not now. I have done this before. I am certain.'

She had a mouthful of cold sloshy egg, but it seemed the wrong time to swallow. Wrong time to move at all. She'd taken the faux skin off her limb, but the metal was nowhere near him. So what was with her belly flipping? The egg demanded to be swallowed. Kira looked away, trying hard not to gag on the sliminess. It was the egg and champers, that was the culprit. It was making her breathe a little weird, too.

'You said you don't know who you are.' She waved a piece of toast towards him.

'I do not.'

'I thought you were a robot.' Kira screwed up her face. 'Fucked if I know now though. You're kind of confusing.'

'A robot.' Blank stare. 'My name is Azrael. Is that a robot name?'

Kira shrugged. 'Blake just called you that. The others kept calling you gallu. Dumb-ass name, it seemed more like your, I dunno . . . your breed or something.'

Azrael the gallu was distracted by a dazzling bracelet

set. Conversation over. Good chat.

A knock at the door interrupted Kira's attempt to stuff a whole piece of toast into her mouth. Azrael glanced up from the sale on chandelier earrings, but she shook her head.

'Nope. Not me, I didn't order anything. I never want to see another bubble again.' She burped to prove the point and got to her feet in a graceless move that saw the toast slide off the plate and land butter-side down on the rug. Whatever. She'd paid a shit-tonne for this room; the cleaners could deal with that.

The cool of the tiled floor snapped at her bare feet. She probably should have put the faux skin back on her arm before she answered the door, but again, whatever. Two female room attendants stood outside, a cart between them, a white cloth covering its contents. They didn't say anything. Just stood there with grins about as genuine as Azrael's first attempt had been.

'I didn't order anything else,' Kira said.

'Complimentary.' The word kind of burst from the nearest woman. She had not a blonde hair out of place and make-up a supermodel would be proud of. The two of them pushed the cart towards Kira, and she stepped out of the way. It was either that or have her bare toes squished. The second woman, with creamy caramel skin and dark hair wound in an intricate braid, closed the door behind her.

'Guys, I said I didn't order anything.' Kira moved to block their path, but the meals-on-wheels team had other ideas.

Braidy-lady shoved the cart forward. It slammed into Kira, knocking her off her feet. Her butt hit the marble floor, and she slid across the polished surface like a failed ice skater. The women turned their attention to Azrael.

'Jesus, Az,' Kira shouted at him. 'Turn the hell around.'

He still had his eyes fixed on the TV, and they were almost on him by the time he reacted. Kira learned a valuable lesson in that instant. Azrael the gallu could get drunk. He stood up and turned, clearly trying to face the attack that came at him from behind the couch, and clearly failing. Like someone who'd just been on a merry-go-round too long, his legs went one way while his top half went the other. He tripped over his own feet and fell backwards. The coffee table didn't stand a chance, shattering beneath him and littering the mauve rug with midnight-black shards. He must have landed on the remote, because suddenly the shopping channel was being shouted at them.

'You are kidding me!' Kira cried.

The only advantage of Azrael's inability to stand on his own two feet was that the two woman were as surprised by it as he was. They faltered, Braidy-lady still behind the couch, Supermodel Susie halfway around the shorter edge of the L-shape. Kira pushed herself to her feet. The cart had a small bain-marie and a couple of dinner plates on it. Judging by the smear of tomato sauce and clinging bow-tie pasta, this was the remnants of someone's dinner. Grabbing one of the plates, Kira flung it, Frisbee style. Her artificial arm was strong. It could make things move like a motherfucker through the air, something she'd discovered throwing a ball for one of the Facility guard dogs. Broke two car windows and pissed everyone off for a week.

Rich red tomato sauce sprayed into the air, and the smell of garlic hit her nostrils hard. But not as hard as the plate hit Braidy-lady. Right in the middle of her back. It would have knocked most people for six, winded them like all hell, but she didn't so much as glance to see where the attack had come from. She just kept going, lifting a leg to clamber over the back of the couch. Supermodel Susie made it round the couch and launched herself at Azrael. It wasn't a pretty sight. Her movements were stiff and jerky, but she landed the strike. Azrael had made it to his knees by this stage, but Supermodel Susie straddled him and he went down again as if she were made of lead.

'Shit, balls, shit.'

Kira grabbed the smooth silver handle of the cart and ran with it, aiming for Braidy-lady. The chick had been one-upped by her own skirt. The form-fitting pencil design was definitely not suitable for clambering over the high back of a leather couch. Cart met leg. The woman screamed, the sound rising over a beer ad blasting out of the overworked speakers, but Kira's attempt to stop her only helped her. The momentum sent her over the back of the couch and tumbling with all the grace of a boneless gymnast onto the seat before she hit the ground, right where Supermodel Susie sat astride Azrael, pinning his arms up over his head. Braidy-lady joined the party, leaning in underneath her companion and planting her hands on Azrael's head. It was one screwed-up game of Twister.

'Fuck's sake, Az. Do something!' Kira shouted over a toilet paper commercial, scanning the room for something she could use to beat the room attendants from hell with. Azrael writhed beneath them. The bitches were average size and weren't using any particularly brilliant ninja moves to keep him down, yet there he was, nailed like a butterfly on a really dodgy pin board. He was wide-eyed. Crazy wide-eyed. She hoped Blake had lodged those ceramic sea-greens in there nice and tight. Way things looked, he might lose them.

'Az, come on! Snap out of it!' Kira screamed over the sound of the TV.

Cutlery had fallen from the cart when she'd rammed it up the woman's ass. A steak knife lay on the floor. Kira grabbed it, then just as quickly dropped it. She was kidding herself if she thought she could stab someone. Even if that someone was perched over her sister's expensive toy like a crow on a mouse. Instead, Kira went for the body slam. She dashed around the couch and slammed herself into the woman astride Azrael. Supermodel Susie landed on top of Braidy-lady. Kira struggled to take a breath, winded by the impact. She wasn't ready for the retaliation, and it was a doozy when it came.

Hands laced around her throat, and she was shoved up against the side of the couch, her back arching over the seat, Braidy-lady's face just a few centimetres from hers. Her breath was foul. Blood poured from the woman's nose. Her grip was all sorts of wrong. It was going to crush the cartilage in Kira's throat. It was definitely making her see stars. This was not how she'd seen this day ending. Black spots grew like mould on her vision. Kira clung to the woman's wrists. The skin there was slick with sweat but cool, as if she'd been sitting under the air-con too long. And there was no chance in hell Kira would dislodge the iron grip.

Holy shit, Kira thought. *Death day is here.* Again. Last time, dying had smelled of smoking brake rubber and her dad's voice telling her to hold on, that it was going to be okay. This time she smelled nothing, and an earnest salesman was telling her she really needed a crystal-encrusted veil for her big day.

It was not going to be okay. There was no breath left. No light. Sounds grew muffled, distant, as if they were coming from the floor below.

Rain sprinkled on her face. At least, something wet did, maybe not rain; Kira was too busy trying not to die to work it out. Something dampened her skin, light like the hydration spray she had in her make-up bag. Maybe it rained in the afterlife. Or they had hydration spray. Kind of handy for hell she supposed.

Hell. Well that wouldn't have been her first choice, but caring took too much energy. She just wanted to drift down, into the quiet dark. Kind of peaceful, this blackness. When she'd killed her dad, it hadn't been serene like this. It had been heat and rancid smells.

A second later, she couldn't feel the woman's hands on her throat anymore. Goodbye cruel world. An additional second later and the world slapped her in the face. It bloody well hurt. Kira took a rushed breath, blinking against light that was determined to blind her. She sucked in more sweet, precious air, breathing like a B-grade porn star.

'What do I do?' someone male and frantic shouted. 'Leona, what do I do?'

The shout was near-deafening, coming from the blur

crouched right beside her. Kira blinked and rubbed at her face, trying to get a clear look. Someone, the shouter, put an arm around her shoulder. He was shaking, and his voice wobbled as he asked her to get up.

'Fuck off,' Kira slurred, attempting to push the blur away.

'Just show him she's all right.' The reply was strained but measured. Female.

'Can you get up?' The shouter stopped shouting, going for a hissed lower tone, but still sounding like he wanted to shit his pants.

Kira squinted, her vision clearing. The guy doing a shitty job of helping her to her feet suffered from a horrendous bowl-cut hairstyle with a fringe that hung low into his eyes, but it was what was beyond the styling disaster that held Kira's attention. Azrael held a woman in a bear hug. An orange blob.

'Oh my god,' Kira said. 'You are fucking kidding me. What are you doing here?'

The tan queen wriggled in Azrael's grasp, her feet a few centimetres from the ground. The very same one Az had knocked senseless in the alleyway at the pub. She looked neither drunk nor leery now, though, in her royal-blue velour tracksuit. She held what looked a hell of a lot like a bubble wand in her right hand. Weird-ass time for blowing bubbles.

'If you don't mind, I'd like to get down now,' the woman said.

'Please, miss.' The boy gave up trying to get Kira to move. 'Could you please tell your friend we aren't here to hurt you?'

He was super young, couldn't have been more than fourteen, Asian, great cheekbones, but his pale skin was dotted with angry acne. The hairstyle was bad enough, but the clothes were just sad. High-waisted jeans with a faded T-shirt emblazoned with some K-pop band tucked into them.

'Kira, are you well?' Azrael said, not seeming to notice the woman's heels slamming into his shins.

'I'm okay, Az.' She levered herself to her feet. Being upright made her head spin. 'You can put her down. Does someone want to tell me what the hell is going on?'

'They are what's going on.' The woman pointed over Kira's shoulder.

The blonde lay directly behind the couch, while Braidy lay closer to the windows. Neither of them was moving, and both were covered in what sure as hell looked like bubbles. Not bubble-bath froth but large translucent orbs, the type kids blew with a slippery solution out of a colourful bottle, the type where the bubble wand was the size of a butterfly catcher, minus the net. The type just like the one the white-haired mess was holding.

'Shit, are they dead?' Murder wasn't great for low profiles. Kira sat down on the edge of the couch; standing made her want to puke.

The boy and the woman, Leona apparently, answered at the same time, both looking mortified it had been suggested.

'Of course not,' Tan Queen Leona sniffed.

'No, no, no,' K-pop boy squeaked.

'What the fuck was their problem?' Kira pressed her fingertips to her temple, as if that could stop the world rocking.

'They have suffered a strong possession, quite unlike one I've seen before.' The woman gave Azrael a sideways look, her expression too hard to read. 'We have subdued them and now will exorcise the spirit within.'

Exorcisms? This little soiree was fast turning into some *Alice in Wonderland* moment.

'And you're doing that how?' Kira indicated the bubble wand. 'With killer bubbles?'

Chances were she was still unconscious. Or dead. Maybe death was down the rabbit hole after all.

The woman patted at some of the wayward strands of her hair, adjusting one of the multiple glittery clips. 'I'm really not appreciating your tone —'

'No?' Kira said. 'Well I didn't appreciate being

strangled, either. We all have burdens to bear.'

Azrael walked over to the woman lying nearest to the windows.

'You're very rude.' Leona might as well have tsk-tsked. 'You should be giving thanks that the Maiden's grace saved you.'

'Maiden's grace? Did your fucking Maiden just grace all over me?' Kira wiped at her damp cheeks. 'It's from those bubbles, right? Do I need to get a shot or something?'

'If you had considered your decision to walk around with a bright one at your side,' Leona jabbed a finger towards Azrael, 'then this conversation would not be necessary.'

Bright one. Clearly she didn't know Azrael all that well.

'Leona,' the boy cried. 'She's moving. She's getting up.'

The 'she' he was referring to was Supermodel Susie. And she wasn't just getting up, she was up and running. Barefoot with a clunky, awkward lope, like one of the walking dead smelling dinner, but it had speed behind it. Her trajectory was odd, though. She wasn't bolting for the door or even one of the other rooms. She was headed across the apartment towards the windows.

'I've got this,' the boy said. 'I've got this.'

The boy didn't look as if he had anything. He rifled around in his pockets. Then he pulled his hand free and flung something from his grasp. Tiny pellets of metal. The dude must have had some muscle behind the swing, because the pellets moved like a swarm of angry wasps across the distance between where he stood and the bolting woman.

She was only about two metres from the window.

'Jesus,' Kira whispered.

Surely windows at this height were shatterproof? She'd bounce off them like a tennis ball. Bit of a concussion, a fractured cheekbone or two.

'Vail, careful. They are too fast!' Leona whipped the wand into the air, producing a stream of shimmering bubbles. She hurled them towards the woman. A bunch of translucent drones on high speed, but the pellets the boy had thrown were already there. Several of them hit the fleeing woman, and she arched her back, looking as though she might fall. She didn't. She jerked herself back into position. Ahead of her the remaining pellets struck the window, and a giant spiderweb of cracks bloomed across it. The boy's scream rose high.

The woman didn't bounce like a tennis ball. She hit the glass and, weakened by the damage already done, the window shattered. Supermodel Susie flew out into the perfect sunny day without a sound. The kid screeched and hollered, either distraught or sickeningly excited about sending someone out a window. Leona shouted at Kira. Telling her it was time to go.

They needed to leave. That a possession that strong probably would have killed the woman anyway.

Probably. A twenty-five storey fall wasn't a probably.

Azrael knelt beside the remaining woman. He cradled her upper body against his chest, gaze shifting between Kira and the gaping, jagged hole in the window.

The only coherent thought that came to Kira's mind centred on how warm the breeze was. The rest was a twisted mess, a half-numb jumble of things that were way too fucked up to deal with in that moment. Someone threw her jacket at her, and she managed to catch it. She didn't recall getting into the elevator. A sobbing boy clung to her most of the way down. She had a vague recollection of Leona telling her to hold him, look after him, while she dealt with getting them out of the hotel unnoticed. Whatever that meant. They weren't exactly an inconspicuous group, even for this town. But the elevator ride made for a very comfortable trip down the rabbit hole. None of that falling down a dirty hole in the back garden crap.

Falling.

Holy shitballs, what the hell had just happened?

She pushed back the thought. Held the kid a little tighter. He clutched a handful of tiny silver pennies. His weapons of choice, the things he'd thrown at the so-dead-now woman, were just coins. Kira had no idea who he was, who the crazy-haired tan queen was either, but here she was anyway. Blake was going to lose her shit. Blend in, Kira. She couldn't have drawn more attention if she'd flashed her clam in the foyer. Kira sought out Az. He was huddled in the corner of the elevator. Emerald-greens lifted. And he didn't need to touch her for her to tell what he was feeling. Shell-shocked. Scared.

Ditto, Kira thought. One arm still wrapped around the sniffling kid, she touched her fingers to her neck. Bruises were a given. She kept her eyes on the elevator's number display and didn't look away till Leona ordered them out of the elevator and into the underground car park.

BLAKE - 15

Blake pushed herself onto her elbows intending to sit up, but Cym was having none of it. Her hands still trembled but nothing like before. And her heart wasn't trying to break her ribs any longer.

'I would not recommend standing just yet.' He leaned in close, tilting his head and shoulders to the right. It seemed an awkward angle that puzzled her until she spotted the camera in the corner of the room. Cym was attempting to shield her. 'You have been unconscious for some time. I convinced them it was due to hypoglycaemia. Your undernourished state lent credence to my diagnosis, but the fault is entirely mine. Your cardiac arrhythmia was quite alarming. Clearly, I exceeded a reasonable level of one of the stimulants and felt that sedation was —'

'How long have I been out?' Blake sank back onto the pillow, staring up at the beige ceiling of the med ward. She did not recall being moved from her apartment. She recalled nothing at all from the moment the black fog had descended on her to the present. Now here she was, in a place she despised more than any other.

'About two hours.' Cym dropped his gaze to the floor. He ran a slender fingertip against his generous lips. 'Some developments have occurred in that time.'

'What is it, Cym? Have they found Kira?' Now Blake did rise, waving back the Syranian when he tried to assist her. Cym had never mastered the marble-hard expressions the others were so adept at. His thoughts were not so easily hidden. 'Tell me.'

But he did not need to.

The double doors to the eight-bed medical ward slid open, and a body on a gurney was wheeled in by two scrub-clad men with masks covering their mouths. Monitoring equipment clung to the end of the gurney, a brunette nurse frowning at it as she assisted the men. Blake recognised her as one who had tended Kira during her time here, but the woman's name escaped her. The group passed by Blake and Cym, but no one so much as glanced their way. Blake grasped Cym's arm, using the leverage to dangle her legs over the side of the bed.

'Oh shit,' she whispered.

Perry lay on the gurney. She stared at the disconcerting

colour of the man's skin. His olive hue had adopted a greenish tinge at his cheeks, with a deeper brown around his closed eyes. The sight did little to steady the low-level trembling working through her limbs. Blake eased herself off the bed, bare feet meeting the coolness of the tiled floor. Black tiles. An odd choice for a medical ward, she'd always thought. But then the Syranians, for whom it was designed, were hardly average patients.

'Take it slowly, Blake.' Cym reached for her, but she cautioned him back with a raised, and visibly shaking, hand.

'I'm fine,' she hissed. She glanced back at the doors. Closed again. No sign of Rossiter. This had most definitely not been the plan, bringing Perry here, but she decided against asking about the bodyguard. Play dumb until she knew more. Perry was alive. Relief and panic mingled within her. That he was breathing was positive, for obvious reasons, but he was also a direct link to Kira – and the airport he'd taken her to.

The men wheeled the gurney into the first compartment on the far side of the room, and on the nurse's count relocated him onto the waiting bed.

'What happened to him, Cym?' Blake rubbed at the puncture marks in the crook of her elbow. The monotonous beep of the monitoring equipment sent chills crawling across the back of Blake's neck. The sound and the room were all-too familiar. When she'd walked out of here three years ago, after Kira had been transferred out of intensive care and up to the ground-level medical facility for recovery, Blake had made it a personal mission never to attend this place again.

Cym's generous lips pressed into a tight line. 'I have not been privy to any information regarding the human.'

'Well, I would like some information.' Blake spotted her boots beneath the bed and leaned down to collect them. 'He looks as if he should be in the hospital. Who gave the order for him to be brought here anyway?'

'That was my directive, Technician. One that does not need to be justified to one such as yourself.'

Blake bolted upright, head spinning with the sudden movement. She pressed a hand into the mattress to steady herself. 'Captain Nex?' Surprise, and not a little dismay, pitched her words.

The captain strode into her glass-walled compartment in his usual determined manner, always appearing to be in a rush to get to his next destination, even if that destination was only paces away. Nex was shorter than several of the Syranians but still a formidable height, and his features were far less soft and feminine than the others. The air of ferocity he carried had taken Blake some time to adjust to. She prided herself on never taking a step back when the captain invaded her personal space.

As he did now.

'Walk with me, Technician. Allow me to show you the result of your stupidity.' The captain's condescension arched his full eyebrows.

Swallowing against a paper-dry mouth, Blake met his gaze. 'I don't understand what you are referring to, Captain.'

Nex tilted his head, and his heavy silver braids shifted against the plating of his black chest armour. 'Is that so? Come.' He turned his back on her and quick-stepped his way across the black tiles to Perry's compartment. Blake followed, as instructed. Nari and Reuben stood guard at the main entrance to the room, a not-so-subtle indication that Blake was both patient and prisoner.

The nurse tending Perry stepped back as the captain approached.

'Where is Azrael, Technician?' The captain moved alongside the bed. 'Where has the Lesser taken him?'

'The Lesser?' Blake said.

'Your sister,' he hissed, moving to stand at Perry's head and bending forward to place his face disconcertingly close to Perry's own. 'Where has Kira taken the gallu?'

The nurse muttered something and hurried out of the room.

'You appear to overestimate the closeness between Kira

214

and I, Captain. I spend most of my time having no idea where my sister is. This is no exception.'

'The fact that your personal guard was located trying to extricate this man suggests this is most certainly the exception.'

The captain touched his lips to Perry's forehead and breathed in so deeply the intake was audible from where Blake stood at the foot of the bed. Nex straightened, pushing up the sleeve on his right arm, revealing the mea stone dug into the flesh. He placed his fingertips in a circle on Perry's forehead, thumb and little finger pressing into his temples. The remaining three digits sank into his dark curly hair. The captain released his breath. The soft sound seemed to go on forever. Blake searched for Cym, but the Syranian had removed himself from the ward. Nari and Reuben stood still as statues at the entrance.

'It is as I suspected.' Nex released his grip, dark marks on Perry's skin where his fingers had pressed. 'You would do well to tell me now where the Lesser has taken the gallu. Other methods we can use to pry the truth from you are far less pleasant than this conversation.'

'I told you, I don't know.' Blake paused. 'Just as we *both* did not know the last time she decided to remove someone from the Facility. What makes you so certain Kira was involved at all?'

The captain turned, head sweeping in a serpentine

flourish to find her. Reminding him of Eron's disappearance was a sure-fire way to rile the Syranian. And right now, anything to distract him while Blake's tired mind tried to come up with a plan was welcome.

'Footage was obtained of Kira entering the gallu's containment area, just prior to the recording being interfered with.'

Blake balled her fists, pressing her ever-trembling hands against her thighs. Weylen's editing abilities were impressive, but also a stark reminder of how deeply Blake had involved her sister in the deception. 'I'll admit, I was made aware of Azrael's removal before advising either yourself or Tamas of the case. Weylen was making her usual checks and discovered the . . . issue. I chose to try to rectify the problem myself. You both were preoccupied with the Final Meld, and I didn't want to disturb your preparations.' The Meldings were teleportation events of some kind, fuelled by the Tier Waters' nuclear-energy-like properties. Certainly not divine occurrences, but the amount of time the Syranians and Tamas spent worshipping their various gods before the events had been useful. 'I sent Rossiter to the Wheel and Barrow; it seemed a logical first choice when I could not locate Kira on Facility grounds. As you know full well, that is where Kira took Eron several times. I had hoped I would find her there again, and Azrael would be returned before any alarm need be raised.'

Perhaps Cym's remedy had actually worsened the effects of the Waters in her veins, because risking the ire of the captain once was foolish. To do it a second time, so blatantly, was insanity. Blake clenched her jaw, the overused muscles there protesting. The captain seemed intent on boring a hole in her skull with his stare, but she'd worked under that gaze long enough to remain visibly unfazed.

'A fine story, Technician. Would not another logical choice have been to locate the vehicle? Or were you hoping I would waste my time and energies doing so?'

'I wasn't aware you knew of the disappearance, but I would have thought Eron would advise you on Kira's adeptness at rerouting the Facility vehicles to suit herself.'

Blake's body rocked, a very slight to and fro, and she hoped the captain's determination to peer beneath her skull distracted him from her instability. He sniffed, the tip of his nose jabbing the air.

'Tell me, what instruction had you given Rossiter regarding the human? What did you intend to do with a human who had suffered a possession by a supermundane? Was your guard taking him to a doctor?'

The smile that curled his lips turned Blake's stomach, but she gave him a disinterested shrug. 'I don't understand what you're talking about. Supermundane?'

'Oh, I believe you know exactly what I'm talking about. You have seen too much evidence of higher beings to deny any longer. The Tier feeds this world once again. This is no longer a godless planet, and the preternatural begin to rise from their long slumber. Fed by the power of the Waters I delivered for our Lord Lahar.'

Blake bit at her lip, hoping her expression didn't betray her desire to slap the smug look from the captain's face. 'I don't know what any of that has to do with Perry. What I saw was a sick man. An epileptic fit perhaps. Cardiac arrest…human shortcomings.'

Because if it were not, then what had happened to him could happen to Kira.

'An utukku possessed this man. The residual indicators are clear, but such a creature has as little time for humans as I do.' Blake had no clue what an utukku was, nor did Nex offer an explanation. Which was fine, so far as she was concerned. Just remaining upright was taking the bulk of her concentration. Nex continued, 'That man was targeted for a reason – the utukku scented the gallu upon him, and hunted through the valleys of the human's mind in search of Azrael. Perry's mind is ruptured beyond repair.' Captain Nex nodded towards the door. The sound of Nari and Reuben's footfalls –

heavy boots reverberating off the concrete floor – reached Blake, but she did not turn around. 'He is dead, you understand? His heart beats at the will of a machine. Even if mere instinct led you to him, your decision to conceal him from us suggests to me you are far from oblivious to your sister's actions. That you know full well where the gallu can be located, and perhaps this man's discovery threatened that. Where have they gone, girl?'

The footsteps ceased, right behind her, but still Blake did not turn around. It was not just her hands shaking now – the trembling went right to the core. And along with it, a sickening, despicable relief that the truth could never be wrung from Perry.

'I do not know.' The words she was least fond of, spoken in a place she despised. 'But I would like to know, as much as you would. Allow me to continue searching for her.'

'You are intelligent, but you are not clever, and you will not win this game, whatever it is you seek to play. Not here amongst the gods and the godly. The reek of fear is strong on you. And rightly so. You've taken something the goddess covets. A terrible move, Technician. You'll be involved in the search, that much is certain. I doubt it will be to your liking, though.' Captain Nex's amusement formed a contorted smile, laced with disdain. He flicked his fingers towards her, as though shooing away a fly. In his mind, he likely was. Reuben took Blake's elbow.

'Let's go, Blake. Tamas is waiting for you.'

Led out of the ward by Tamas's bodyguards, Blake searched once more for Cym. But found only the frightened face of the nurse who had attended Perry.

Reuben was not gentle as he shoved Blake into Tamas's room but she made certain not to give any indication of the discomfort. The guards left them alone. If ever there was someone who looked as drained as Blake felt, it was Tamas. His olive skin was stormy and bruised beneath his eyes. He sat on the edge of his unmade bed. Once upon a very long time ago, they'd shared that bed, both regretting the encounter while the sheets were still damp. Tamas's taste for men had been fortified, and Blake had learned without doubt she shared none of Kira's obsession with bodily contact. The messy, revealing thing that it was. There'd been no one before, no one since. And no desire to change the status quo.

Inexplicably though, the relationship with Tamas had deepened. The silences they shared had lengthened. And when conversation did occur, he never remonstrated her when she sank into her thoughts, oblivious to the company she shared. They were perfect at being utterly disconnected, together.

But there was no oblivion now. No silence. Tamas stared at the flat-screen TV on the wall opposite his bed.

'You've done a wonderful job, Blake,' he said softly. 'I knew you would. I wish my mother could see this. I'd make her eat each and every patronising word she spat at me when I chose you. She was an overbearing bitch. I do not miss her, but I'd endure a moment in her company if it meant she could witness this.'

The footage was of level eleven and the four carapaces Blake had led a team in creating. They dangled from four miniature cranes assembled around the Tier. These four had none of the sculpted beauty of Azrael. An odd compulsion had seen Blake remove all softness from their design and replace it with adamantine detail, fashioning the bodies on the thick set of a conditioned soldier and the blocky presence of a rugby player. Two males, two females. Intimidating, perhaps even frightening. She'd etched her own natural warning into their construction, like the blue rings on a deadly octopus, or the red stripe on the back of a spider.

Be warned. Stay away.

Blake bit the inside of her cheek, reopening a barely healed wound there. She may not adhere to the idea that the gods toyed with the world, but there was no denying the power of the technologies involved, and her own obsession with learning their secrets. Blake owed the Syranians Kira's life, but she had never been totally blind to the dangers. The designs of the four hunters were her red flags to the world.

Tamas patted the mattress. 'Come, sit with me, Blake.'

'Tamas, I do not know where Kira has taken Azrael. I honestly do not.' Blake sat down, the give of the mattress rocking her against Tamas. He laid his hand on her thigh, a physicality he'd not displayed since their ill-fated lying together, and his touch did now what it had not done then. Sent heat spreading through her body.

'Blake, we have known each other a very long time. Well before we became so much more than we'd ever been. Do you remember that we used to share tinned beans in university? You always took the larger portion, but I didn't care. I truly didn't.' The reeds in the garden beyond the floor-to-ceiling windows swayed back and forth beneath a clear morning sky. Insects darted at the still surface of the water. 'Because you were my friend. A companion who had as many idiosyncrasies, and as few friends, as I did. And it is that history that enables me to offer you one last chance. Tell me where they have gone.' His fingers dug into her thigh, nails pushing at the thin material of her black pants.

In the haze of fatigue, and duress, and whatever else swirled through her system, Blake wavered. The captain had told her she would not win this game. Highly likely, considering she wasn't sure what game she was playing. Arrogance had driven her to begin with. They had wanted to take Azrael from her, to destroy her creation when they were done with it. Like a disposable toy. But that motivation had shifted as she'd watched Perry die. She'd recalled a particular book in her possession. One her father had presented her with, just a year before the accident. A copy of the Bhagavad Gita, the very same text Oppenheimer had quoted after the dropping of the atomic bomb. *'I am become death, destroyer of worlds.'*

All because she'd told him of a new development in drone tech that the Facility was pioneering. Her father had had no knowledge of the aliens, no inkling of the superiority of their technology. No clue of what she would become involved in. A simple drone had pressed him to declare his own daughter in danger of becoming a monster. Blake had despised him for it. Abhorred his lack of vision. Didn't speak to him for weeks. The book had been propping up her lopsided fridge ever since.

Tamas drew in closer, his breath warm against Blake's skin. 'One chance. Or I will make you hurt the same way I was made to hurt when the goddess learned Azrael was gone.'

What would her father think now? She had to keep playing. No matter the game.

Blake pressed her mouth up close to Tamas's ear. 'I

don't know where they are.'

Tamas slammed his hand on the comms unit beside the bed. 'You can come in.' He stood up, pacing away to the far side of the room and standing with his back to her, eyes fixed on the garden his mother had built.

The entrance slid open and Cym entered. A brief moment of relief faded when he refused to meet her gaze. He did not look at her as he rolled up her sleeve and his firm grip left her no option but to hold still as he swabbed her arm.

'What are you doing?'

'Let it be done, Blake.' Tamas kept his back to her. 'You'll tell us what we need to know.'

Cym removed a needle from a satchel at his hip. He pushed the needle against her skin and before he broke the surface, leaned towards her and whispered, 'Forgive me.'

Blake wrenched against his grip, panic knotting her chest. She had pre-planned for this contingency. The use of a truth agent. Human wars were full of such chemical weapons, odds were high that the aliens used them too. But had she done enough to protect herself? An icy sensation raced up her arm, pushing goosebumps to the skin's surface. That soon changed. Ice became fire, pincers of glowing embers reaching into her skull. Blake screamed, clawing at her ears. She fell to her knees, but Cym dragged her back to her feet, pinning her hands behind her back. Arching her back, slamming her head against his chest, Blake sought some, any, relief from the agony. The screams overflowed from her mouth, choking her. How had she ever supposed she could withstand this?

'Don't fight it,' Cym hissed into her ear. Each word a new flame. A new searing horror. 'Let go and it will not pain you. Let it take you.'

Tamas stepped in front of her. Blake kicked out. Or, at least, tried to lash out. A straightforward enough movement in her head, but there was no response from her body. Liquid flowed down her face, cool against her blazing skin.

'Where did you send them, Blake?' Tamas stood with his hands clasped behind his back, regarding her the same way he had the garden. 'This can be over very quickly.'

The words forming at the back of her throat ran along the lines of *fuck off*. But what fell from her mouth was far worse.

'Melgrove,' she screamed. 'I sent them to Melgrove, cabins on the north side of town. We were all supposed to go for Kira's twenty-first birthday, and I never showed. I was here. I hate myself for that.' It was a horrifying torrent pouring from her, dragging her far too close to what she sought to hide. Blake's scream tore at her vocal chords, and in desperation she reached for one undeniable truth. 'But that was nothing, compared to what she did. She took him away from us. It was her fault, not mine. I wasn't there. I wasn't there. I was never there. I am never there. But it was not my fault. She killed him. Not me.'

Blake rocked back against Cym, damning them all to silent hell. Whatever serum Cym had injected her with, it plucked almost all of the truth out of her, like a crow on a carcass. The shouting match she'd had with Kira, the fury in her sister's voice as she demanded to know why Blake was cancelling on them again, had rung in her head for three years.

'Can you contact her, Blake?'

'No. No. I can't. She's alone. I've left her all alone. But I couldn't . . . I just can't . . . I can't stand to look at her sometimes. She looks just like them. Like them both. And I miss them so much. But they would hate . . . hate me . . . my mother would hate what I've done. I've left her all alone.'

Razors, each and every word, bursting out of the black space she'd hidden them in, filling her mouth. She screamed. The sound rose up out of her diaphragm and engulfed her. Hands clamped around her face. Someone was shouting, their words muffled beneath the weight of the terrible cries jackhammering her ribs. A sting at her elbow and her mouth clamped closed. Blake slumped against Cym. The Syranian wrapped his long limbs tightly around her, muttering soft reassurances against the back of her head.

Tamas crouched on his knees by the window. With one hand pressed to the glass, he rose to unsteady feet. 'We are done. I will inform the captain. Take the time you need, tidy her up. Get her back on her feet.' Tamas moved as though to approach, but reconsidered and stopped in the middle of the space dividing them. Blake blinked through the tears that still fell unbidden. If not for Cym's support, she would slither to the floor, her legs jelly.

'We have become so much more than we've ever been, Blake.' Tamas echoed his earlier words. 'I want you to truly see that. You'll finish what you've started. I need you to . . . you will be there at the Final Meld. You are the Technician, and your expertise will be required. What becomes of you after that, I can't say. You've taken that out of my hands, but you will fill your role at the Meld. You will do it. If you don't want Kira hurt, you'll do it.'

Blake fought to place her lips around a reply. Tamas was halfway out the door when she finally managed to slur a response.

'We are less than . . . we've . . . ever . . . been.'

KIRA - 16

Kira's head was full of questions, and her bladder full of champagne. If Leona-the-bubble-wonder drove over another pothole, chances were the newspapers and magazines filling the footwells of the car were going to get a soaking. The baby-blue Datsun station wagon's suspension was nonexistent. And, judging by the way Kira's butt sagged into the crease between the backrest and the cushion, so were the springs in the back seat. Az rested his feet on a pile of old papers so high it raised his knees above his waist. He clutched the seat in front, which, considering the snail's pace they drove at, seemed overly cautious.

'Where exactly are we going?' Kira asked for the third time in about as many minutes.

Leona had spent the better part of the drive trying to get a word out of the kid with the terrible bowl cut. But Vail wasn't talking. At least he wasn't bawling his eyes out and dribbling words anymore. There was a little damp patch just above Kira's left boob where the kid had huddled against her all the way down to the car. He was taller than Kira, which meant he'd kind of hunched over her. Couldn't have been great for his neck but it had taken a few tugs to get him to let her go when they'd reached the car. His pockets jingled as he moved. Each one seemed to be full of coins. All the way down in the elevator he'd kept babbling about something called 'workings'. His workings had been too strong. They had never been too strong before apparently. He hadn't meant to hurt her.

The girl, not Kira.

Well, his fault or not, the girl who'd hurtled out the window was dead as a fucking dodo. Kira twisted in her seat, staring out over the flat back of the wagon. It was filled with crap, too: papers, boxes, a pair of hiking boots, a few folding chairs, a couple of bundles of sticks, an empty fish tank. Great. They were on the run with the world's greatest car hoarder. Something smelled weird, like burnt Christmas cake. No one liked fruit cake, especially in a car with no air-con. This day was just getting better and better. Kira peered over the piled-up junk to the road behind them. If she saw flashing lights, she really was going to piss herself.

'We're not being followed.' Leona said. 'No one will

recall us, not for a little while.'

'You sound pretty sure.'

'I am more than pretty sure,' Leona sniffed. 'It's not my first indifference incantation, girl.'

It wasn't her first missed gear change, either. The crunch sounded like a metal alligator taking a bite out of the engine. One more of those babies and this pile of shit would give it up. *This crazy bitch ain't driving us any further,* the car would say in Car-talk-ese. Wow. Kira blinked – she was tired.

Crunch, screech, fucking crunch.

'Jesus, you're killing this thing, lady,' Kira said.

'Would you like to drive?'

'No. No I wouldn't.' Few things in life were certain. Kira not ever getting behind a wheel again sure as fuck was.

'What's your name, girl?' Leona stared straight ahead, keeping an all-too-polite distance from the car in front.

'Kira.' Shit. So much for super-undercover secret squirrel.

'Well, Kira, I'd like you to shut your ungrateful mouth if you wouldn't mind.'

Kira considered using her ungrateful mouth to tell the tan queen where to shove it. But quickly decided against it. Whatever that bullshit was back at the hotel, Tan Queen and Bowl-cut boy might have just saved her ass.

'Fine,' she said. 'But can this ungrateful mouth ask you where we're going?'

'It can, but I don't have any answer. Didn't exactly plan on this.'

'You and me both, sister,' Kira said.

Sister.

Blake.

Jesus. Now that was a call Kira didn't want to make. And right now, it was a call she couldn't make. Kira sat upright, patting at the obviously empty pockets on her leather pants. No credit card, no phone. Most naked she'd ever been.

'Fuck,' she said. 'Does anyone have a phone?'

'Vail does but it's no use to you now, I'm afraid,' Leona declared with far too much perkiness. 'Not with the level of workings in that room. Fried the circuits. I think I saw smoke rising from the back of that television. Did you not notice that we had blessed silence in the end? No more dreadful advertisements.'

Kira rested back against the seat. 'Nope, was kind of busy.'

Up ahead, the traffic light shifted to orange. Leona could have floored it and gotten through without much fanfare. Nope. She brought the car to a neat stop and pulled on the handbrake. This was not how dramatic getaways rolled in the movies. The smell of burnt herbs, cinnamon maybe, niggled at the inside of Kira's nose. In the ashtray between the driver and passenger, there was a small clump of sticks tied with a fine red string.

'You know what,' Kira said, 'I really think we should get out.'

The woman regarded her in the rearview, her eyes partly hidden behind wayward strands of stark-white hair.

'Oh, okay then,' Leona said. 'So you're fine with being strangled again by possession spirits? Because they will come for him.'

Kira eyeballed her back. 'I'm asking you nicely to let us out.'

'I'm asking you nicely if you have the faintest idea that you're walking around with a bright one.'

The light flicked to green, but Leona didn't press the accelerator. The car behind did one of those polite but clear move-the-fuck-on toots of its horn.

'No need to be a sarcastic bitch,' Kira said. 'Az is just a little slow.'

Kira didn't like it. Didn't like it at all, the way Leona stared at Az every time she had a chance. Azrael was oblivious. He was still in some kind of mute mode. Hadn't uttered a single word since they'd gotten in the car. Maybe he was still drunk.

Or maybe he felt like she did. Like someone had just thrown her into a screwed-up reality game show with a fucked-up premise – *Roll up, roll up, get nearly deaded, watch someone die, run away and hope like a motherfucker no one saw you.*

'You can't see him at all, can you?' Leona interrupted Kira's game-show storyboarding. 'He's as bright as the sun, girl, and you have no clue at all.'

Another less polite toot from behind and Leona shifted into gear and pulled the car out into the intersection.

'I can see him just fine.' Kira pressed a hand to her belly. 'Look, I'd really like to get off the crazy bus now.'

Car sickness wasn't a problem. Not normally. But Kira's insides weren't behaving. A crack in the vinyl seat poked at her ass no matter where she shifted, and she was pretty sure she'd pissed her pants a little. She glanced down at herself. And sighed. Realising for the first time since bolting that she didn't have the faux skin on her arm. Armadillo was plain for all to see. Way to go incognito. At least the prosthetic didn't seem to ring any bells for these two.

'Say I let you out here, just drop you off at the nearest Taco Bell. Then what?' A toss of white hair, a bob of cheap plastic hair clips. 'You weren't doing so well dealing with the supermundanes back there. I'm guessing that whoever you are, you don't know any wardings or incantations.'

'There was nothing super about those crazy fucking cows. And I have the only incantation I need.' Access to the Facility. That vapid concrete hell seemed like fucking heaven right now.

'Ah, but we can offer you the protection of the Maiden. Something I very much believe you are going to need.'

So the woman thought of herself as some kind of killer bubble-blowing witch. Maybe one of the long sticks in the back was her broom. Happy days.

'Definitely time for us to leave you.' Kira grabbed the door handle, intending to rattle it. The handle came free in her hand. 'You're fucking kidding me. Stop the damn car. Now.'

Vail chose then to show signs of life. He turned in his seat to face her, eyes red-rimmed from crying, the end of his nose damp and glistening with snot.

'Kira, it's okay. We mean well,' he said. 'Let us help you. I'm not sure you know what's around you, what those things were.'

His own internal memory of 'those things' seemed to jab at him. He flinched, pale as all hell. And Kira couldn't bring herself to tell him what she really thought of his offer to help. It would be like yelling at a teddy bear. And the kid had had a fucking awful day. But she was tired of this party. She wanted to go home. Surely this wasn't what Blake had in mind. Death while babysitting?

Taking a breath, Kira focused on Vail. 'I have somewhere I can go. Somewhere they can deal with this. So thank you, for whatever you did back there, but we need to go.'

She needed to pee like a racehorse. Needed a drink right after that. Azrael shifted beside her, trying to find more space for his feet amongst the papers. Kira glanced at him, about to ask him what his problem was when a flash of black caught her eye. Small, fast, and down near her foot.

'Rat, a fucking rat.' Kira hurled herself back in her seat, pushing her butt towards the door. With the jerk of her body weight against it, the handleless door decided to open.

'Fucking Jesus!' Kira yelled.

Magazines and newspaper spilled out onto the road.

'Pull over, Leona. Pull over!' Vail shouted.

She shouted right back. 'I'm not blind!'

Someone grabbed Kira's flailing arm and pulled. Hard. She slid across the cracked vinyl seat as if it were covered in oil, colliding with Azrael. The dude might as well have been a brick wall. Leona jerked the car to a stop.

'What was all that about?' she demanded.

'Your car is shit.' Kira pulled away from Azrael's grip, kicking at the junk in the footwell. 'And it's got rats.'

'You bloody stupid girl,' Leona glared. 'There are no

rats in this car.'

'I saw a fu . . .' Kira froze.

Leona was right. There were no rats. But there was something. Perched on Azrael's knee. A blob of ugly orange and black.

'Lizard. Fucking lizard. Get it off him.' Kira waved her hands near it, not about to try to touch the thing.

'Bradley,' Leona exclaimed, 'for all the Maiden's braids, what are you doing here?'

The little critter was tiny, but Kira'd seen the way geckoes at the Facility moved. So fucking quick. You had no clue where the little bastards were going. Up your jeans, or under your bedsheets, maybe even into your earhole during the night. Kira shuddered. Disgusting. And this one looked like it had dressed up for Halloween. The folds of skin on its head gave it the look of a mini Triceratops. Its body was pitch black, save for a strip of orange down the centre of its back, flanked by two lines of paler orange dots. Eyes like lumps of coal. It stared up at Azrael, ignoring Kira's fluttering fingers completely.

'Don't touch it, Az. Some of these fuckers are poisonous,' Kira said.

And apparently hypnotising. Az stared at the thing. And the thing stared back.

Vail threw his door open and raced around to open the door alongside Azrael.

'Bradley? Are you okay?' he said.

The reptile turned its bulbous head and bulgy eyes and flicked a pink tongue towards the boy before turning back to Azrael, who tilted his head in mimicry. Thankfully, his tongue stayed in his mouth. He used it instead to speak.

'What is this?'

For whatever bizarre reason, it still gave her a buzz, hearing his voice. Like a proud mumma with a two-year-old. Leona's drawn-on eyebrows lifted. 'So you have a voice.'

'It's just a lizard, Az,' Kira said. 'It's not going to hurt you.'

'No. It is not.' Azrael's lips did a weird snaking thing. He just wasn't nailing the smiling thing.

Vail crouched down beside the car. 'Bradley is a *Tylototriton anguliceps*, a newt. Extremely rare. But he is supposed to be in his tank in the lounge room at home. What's going on, little guy?'

The little guy, all twenty or so centimetres of him, let out a squeaky bark, like an especially tiny chihuahua, and scurried across Azrael's lap.

'Shit, it's moving.' Kira pushed herself across the vinyl. 'I'm out.'

But Bradley the newt had no interest in her. Or Azrael. It leapt towards the boy, landing in Vail's outstretched hand. He whispered to the slimy reptile before placing it on his shoulder. Kira stepped out of the car, blinking. Damn it was bright. The metal of her arm did its usual thing; soaking in the sunlight, turning the glow into something flat and matte. She used the armadillo to shade her eyes and try to get some idea of where they were. Leona had parked them in a car park, disused if the weed-infested cracks were anything to go by.

'Az, get out of the car,' she said. 'We need to go. Leona, thanks for helping us not die back there. We'll catch you guys later. Az —' She turned. He was right there, blocking the light. 'Shit, Az —'

He took her hand. Metal hand. Kira sucked in her breath. Bracing. But it was gentler this time. A subtle jolt, a rush of all things prickly and nice, a hum that turned her to mushy, tingly jelly. She wondered briefly if her bladder would hold out, then her thoughts were all Azrael. Not sentences or even words, nothing so pronounced. It was all just understanding, certainty, like knowing that you wanted chocolate over caramel.

He wasn't going to leave.

He was frightened.

No. Kira frowned. A different kind of scared. Not like

he'd been about the Facility. This time he was frightened of loss. Kira sighed against the gooeyness. Hard to focus when your whole body tingled like it was about to come. Losing what? She didn't know how this worked, but maybe if she threw out a thought, he'd throw something back.

Stay.

Clear as a bell.

Stay.

Azrael wanted to stay with these weirdos. And his desperation made her chest ache. Lost.

The 'bright one' was so damn lost the backs of her eyes prickled with tears.

'Oh Jesus.' Kira pulled her hand free. Screw that shit. She drew the line at tears. Kira cradled the armadillo against her chest.

Azrael stayed right where he was. Too damn close. Watching her the way a dog did when you had a bone in your hand. Leona and Vail weren't much better. Eyes wide. Mouths open. Like she'd actually just fucked Az in the middle of the abandoned car park.

The only one who didn't eyeball her as if she were the main act in a freak show was the reptile. Newt. Triceratops. Fucking whatever. Bradley jumped from his perch on Vail's shoulder, disappearing into the car and squawking his miniature lungs out. As if he already knew what was going to happen next. Christ, this was a bad idea.

'Get back in the car, Az.'

TAMAS - 17

As he neared the level eleven chamber, the force of the Tier Waters rushed at him. Tamas stumbled. In danger of falling to his knees, he grabbed at the rough surface of the passageway walls, wincing as the stone jabbed the flesh of his palm. Reuben moved to assist, but Tamas waved him back.

'I'm fine.' He heard the rasp in his own voice but was grateful for Reuben's discreet step back, a move so fast that no one might notice he'd tried to help at all. 'Give me a moment.'

Either he'd grown weaker – possible – or the Waters sensed what was coming. Their energy already stirred, brutal against his raw nerves. Tamas had attempted to rest since the incident with Blake, but her screams blared through his skull, making deep sleep impossible. Over and over he saw the truth torn from her like jagged blades, the first time he'd witnessed the use of the Syranian serum. Her pain had weighed down the room. She'd been stripped to the core.

And it had dragged him to the ground.

Thinking of his collapse burned his cheeks even now. It was pathetic. He was Ereshkigal's Messenger. In his veins ran the strength of demigods, the very last echoes of the blood of the Abgal: seven sages created by Enki, the god of knowledge. An extraordinary family legacy.

A legacy gifted to a stuttering, trembling mess of a human. The man who could barely stay on his feet as he went to do his goddess's bidding. Who lay awake at night, so sick with worry that he would screw all this up. *Not strong enough.* His mother might as well have been lying with him some nights, her voice so clear in his head. If that serum were used on him, what might they see? He was not certain what he feared most: that they would see his weakness, his fear, or the hint of a monster. A monster who had allowed the torture of the single human he called friend, and who wasn't sure that, for some time at least, he hadn't enjoyed the power play.

Tamas straightened, adjusting the button-up shirt he'd chosen, and continued his walk down the hallway. The grand arching doors to the level eleven chamber were visible up ahead. He cleared his throat. 'Any word on the location of the gallu?'

The back of his skull ached not just from the incident

with Blake. A headache had plagued him since he'd advised Ereshkigal of Azrael's disappearance. It was impossible to gauge the goddess's emotion; it was a little like communicating with a voice-command system, but suffice to say, she was not pleased at the loss. He didn't need another reason to despise Kira. The list was long. She was a bully, careless, irresponsible. Reckless with her freedom. Trivial. Coarse and irreverent.

All things he'd envied to begin with. Jealous of her utter nothingness.

'No, sir. They are still en route to Melgrove,' Nari informed him, keeping a discreet distance. 'Another hour until touchdown.'

'And you've still not been able to reach the accommodations?'

Reuben shook his head. 'The number goes direct to voicemail.'

A goddess in his head, alien technology at hand, and Tamas could not find a way to reach the manager of a rundown holiday park. He sucked in a deep breath. Held it. Exhaled, giving his heart a chance to stop pounding.

Chances were Ereshkigal already saw his truth. Already knew the words that would bubble out of him. That he lusted for and feared, in equal measure, what lay ahead. He'd been promised that the full power of the Abgal would be reborn within him should he bring the soul of Dumuzi to her. That Enki himself would reward Tamas by restoring the bloodline of the sages to its full glory. Thoughts of that grand prize kept him awake at night.

Be careful what you wish for, so the saying went. And he'd never understood it so well.

Tamas gestured to the men standing guard at the heavy, imposing doors. No eye contact. As protocol dictated. But right now, as the interior door swung open and the blast of the Waters met him, Tamas had the oddest fleeting desire. He wished it was the janitor standing before him. Too inquisitive, too invasive of personal space, too eager to chat with the messed up boy who might be about to disappear altogether.

He strode past the men and into the chamber. The air was heavy, clogging his airways. They were all there. All the Syranians to the right, standing to attention behind their captain. Cym included, and Eron. The most elegant, and by far the prettiest of all the Syranians. Something beautiful to look at in the drabness of the Facility. He'd filled more than a few of Tamas's fantasies, until he'd slept with Kira.

Tamas gestured for his escort to stop.

'Here will be fine.' His entire body shook. Sweat beaded on his lip. The starched collar of his favourite dot-patterned shirt clung too tightly to his neck.

Nari looked as if she might say something. A 'good luck' or a 'be careful', perhaps. It would have made him sweat with the intimacy of it, but it would have been nice just the same. No one else in here was going to wish him anything but to get the job done. Nari gave him a deep nod and then walked away. Reuben went a little further, giving a very brief salute. Then he, too, was turning his back and walking away. Tamas searched for a sign of Blake, scanning the huge chamber. Sound echoed against the dark upper curves, playing around the stalactites that dotted the roof, hanging like enormous blades, ready to strike them all down.

Four smart-rig mini cranes were positioned around the perimeter of the Tier. They were yellow and red, the only splashes of bright colour amongst the stark-white rock and dull concrete flooring of level eleven. Each crane sat like a crab on four braced legs, a tractor tyre beneath the core hub. A thick curved steel arm held a completed carapace. Four lifeless human constructs dangled from thick wire rigging, each as different as humans were in actuality. Varying sexes – two female forms, two male – and skin shades. Blake stood by the male on the farthest side of the Tier, a laptop in her hand connected by wires to the monitoring unit at the head of the crane. The stark white of her skin seemed to glow with the reflection of the Waters. The body that hung before her dwarfed her small frame, like a football player before a child. It was the same for the three others. Azrael's slender physique, the refined beauty of it, was missing in these designs. The Four were bulky and imposing. Like the bouncers at the clubs Tamas never went to.

A sudden pain at his crown almost doubled him over. It took every ounce of effort to keep it to nothing more than an odd-looking twitch. The goddess was impatient. Tamas turned to Captain Nex, who stood waiting a few paces away.

'We are ready, Messenger.' His white eyes fixed on Tamas's face. Not a hint of trepidation. No doubt. Tamas envied the surly captain for the first time. 'Shall I give the order?'

He nodded, the air evaporating from his lungs. 'Yes,' he said. Whispered.

Seder, Bel, Gren, and Parator moved in that silky way they had, one in behind each of the cranes. One to each of the Four. Ready to Bind. Connect the mea stones they bore in their arms with the sister stones worked into the carapaces. The aliens used the mea stones like extrasensory lassoes, not only to connect them to the gallu but also to control them. Keep each of the Four set on one task: find the demigod. They would search amongst hundreds of thousands of humans and find the single body that contained the eternal soul of Dumuzi.

Ereshkigal's gallu were the only beings capable of doing so, they were the ones who had bound him to human flesh to begin with. But they were wild animals and would fight their restraints every step of the way.

A drop of sweat ran down the side of his face. The Syranians all appeared utterly calm, portraying the perfect soldierly resolve. Not a bead of sweat or quickened breath.

Nothing like him.

'Cym and the Technician are ready to commence?' Tamas avoided the captain's intense gaze. As with all the Syranians, he held an imposing height and was lean and tightly wound. Tamas always felt the captain could swipe off your head before you realised he'd lifted a hand. The alien was yet another intimidating presence around him. Tamas seemed to draw such people to him. As though they fed on his vulnerability. Even his mother had enjoyed lording over him. She had been a Messenger of the goddess before all else, reminding him of that fact on every occasion possible. There was no room for crayon drawings on fridges in his childhood.

'I believe so, Mr Cressly.' Always a hint of condescension when the captain spoke his name. If Nex were a gambler, he would have put down a hefty sum against Tamas surviving this far. 'Though I've made clear my opposition to including Blake in the Meld.'

'You have indeed.' He hid his shaking hands, bunching them up under his armpits. An unobtrusive move considering the chill of the chamber. He sought out Blake, willing her to look up from the tablet she cradled. Her eyes stayed steadfastly down. 'And I've made clear the fact that her expertise is required. Cym agrees. He will be in the control room and needs someone out in the chamber. Believe me, Captain, Blake understands the consequences of any lack of cooperation. The Taser restraints I've had put on her bodyguard should go some way to clearing up any misunderstandings, should her memory fail her.'

Reuben's idea. So that not only did Kira's well-being rely on Blake cooperating, but Rossiter's did too. Considering they were clearly the only two people in the world Blake gave a damn about, bases were covered. A knife pierced through his cerebellum, the clawing grip of the goddess. Tamas flinched, gasping with the shock of the pain.

'We must start,' he said – or, chances were, his eyes would start to bleed. 'I will give the Technician the go-ahead.'

There was absolutely no reason to walk the twenty paces it would take to reach Blake's side. Raise one finger and he had people at his beck and call who would tell her to prepare. Besides, not a single soul in the chamber was unaware the Meld was about to commence. He saw the darted glances, the tension in the expressions around him. But Blake would not look up. And he needed her to look up. Look at him. See him. Before he disappeared.

Someone she'd given a shit about once. Someone who regretted tearing open her soul. And who despised himself for being grateful it had not been him.

'We are ready to commence.'

Blake's head jerked up, and he knew it had been a mistake to come this close. 'I know.'

As if he were a steaming pile of shit.

'All right, then.' Tamas fought the urge to cradle his head in his hands, try to ease the headache pressing the backs of his eyes. Blake pulled the wires free of the monitoring unit, bundling them around the tablet, and raised her gaze to meet him. The delicate skin beneath her eyes was bruised and sunken. A vein bulged at her temple, easily visible through her pale skin.

His throat tightened.

She did not see a friend. Did not even see someone she could stand to be around. Though the chamber itself was noisy with the hum of voices and whir of machinery, a bubble of silence sat around them. As though they stood behind heavy curtains, blocked off from everyone else. And in the silence, Tamas waited. Blake's hands shook. Just as his did.

'Have you found them?' Blake said. 'Is Kira all right?'

Fuck. Fuck. Tamas gritted his teeth. Fury pressed down on his ribs, making it hard to breathe. Is that stupid bitch all right? Of all the questions. Inside, down in a space he couldn't pinpoint, something broke. Tamas reached for Blake, grasping her blouse and jerking her forward. She cried out, the tablet slipping from her grasp and clattering to the floor.

'I found them.' The words hissed from him. 'And if you put one finger out of line, I will tear her apart. I'd like to see her full of the serum. Killing your own father has got to pack one hell of a punch, right? I'll fill her so full of her truth, she'll die screaming.' He pushed her away. The full force of his anger propelled her backwards, landing her flat on her back. He panted with the effort, the rage tearing through him. Bloating him. Building him into something so much grander than he was. Blake and her secrets could go to hell. The death at the casino was a flashing red light. Kira would be in his possession soon enough.

Blake pushed up onto her elbows but did not try to stand. The jolt had loosened strands of her dark hair, and the top button of her blouse had torn free. Her collarbones poked through thin skin, the curve of her ribs visible. He was not the only one disappearing.

'Tamas, what are we doing?' Blake whispered. 'How

many are going to be hurt?'

Tamas was conscious of the eyes on him, but he didn't flinch. Didn't blush. Didn't give a shit. He kicked the tablet towards her. Its harsh scrape across the concrete surface was the only sound that reached him. The entire chamber silent. Even the headache had lifted. As though the goddess herself had backed off.

'Oh come on, Blake, when has that mattered to you? Don't expect me to believe you've grown a conscience now. Bullshit. Your designs bring in millions.' He gestured to the grimalkin standing at the perimeter of the chamber. The military had paid a ridiculous amount of coin for similar designs. 'This is just a different kind of war.' He laughed, the sound rich with scorn. 'That's what the whole thing with Azrael is, right? You don't want them to take your toys away from you. Good luck with hiding him. Believe me, this world isn't big enough for that.'

He turned his back on her, ignoring her pleas to stop. To wait. Her assistant Weylen was the first to move, giving him a wide berth as she ran to Blake's side.

Tendrils of energy stroked him, caressed him far more gently than when he'd entered the chamber. Luring him towards the Tier. Ereshkigal flowed into his mind, with far less of a hammer blow than before. A pressure not altogether comfortable, but not about to level him, either. Tamas nodded to the captain, who waited at the crude low brick wall around the Tier.

Captain Nex called out readying orders to his god-soldiers. Eron remained a step behind his captain. His silver hair was pulled tight off his face, accentuating the sharp lines of his features. His lips parted, the fullness of them glistening against the shimmering Waters. It would have been quite breathtaking if not for the drift of his pale white eyes. He could barely pull his gaze from where Blake was being helped to her feet by Weylen.

Even though Tamas stood a pace away, his body alight with the power of the goddess, Eron could not gift him with so much as a glance. To hell with them all.

'Let it begin.'

Fully clothed, Tamas stepped into the Waters. And no one offered him a single word. He stood, calf-deep, on the narrow concrete platform that ran around the inner rim of the Tier. The atmosphere in the chamber grew weighty, pressing in on him like a wet blanket. He would not bend to it today. He was upright, rigid. Outwardly unafraid. The four carapaces dangled over the Waters, the cranes emitting a low hum as they slowly lowered the bodies closer to the surface of the liquid. He moved down a few more steps, reaching the jutting platform that would allow him to walk to the centre of the Tier. The Tier was not overly large, half the size of an average swimming pool. The bodies hung above him, crowding in on him, adding to the oppressive dankness of the air.

The Waters began to swirl, and with each rotation they grew more viscous. Heat poured through his body as the Waters rose up his legs, covering his torso. Tamas glanced up but caught sight of no one. Only the empty shells hanging lifeless around him. He was alone – save for the deity in his brain. His body swelled, any wrinkles he may have had were stretched clear. The Waters covered his eyes. Drenching him. Drowning him. Calling to his blood.

His blood called back, pulsing as thick as the Waters in his veins. The spasms began soon after. Tamas clenched his teeth, fingernails cutting into his swollen, curled fists. Azrael's Meld was a toothache compared to this. Tamas knew from the tightness in his throat and the wideness of his open mouth that he was screaming, but he heard nothing. It was complete and utter silence, the most frightening thing of all. His connection to the world had been deadened into nothingness. Vision was gone, lost beneath a blur of emerald. Taste, smell, the sense of the Water against his skin, all gone. He was nothing. He was no one and nowhere. A consciousness masquerading as light. It, he, guided them, pulled them in, dragged them forward. A beacon to lead them.

And they were everything and everywhere.

The Four.

At the eye of their storm Tamas struggled to exist. Losing himself in the maddened rush of ascendancy, eroding. Brilliance moved around him, achingly bright. Buffeting him in the storm of arrival.

All at once the crashing wave dumped him. He choked on the Waters pouring down his throat, gagging so hard that bile filled his mouth. His ears screamed with the pitch of tinnitus, and the concrete steps rushed up to meet him. Slammed against him.

The Tier was done with him. The goddess was done with him. And he cried into the wetness.

BLAKE - 18

A light mist drifted off the mass of moving water, dampening everyone, and everything, in the chamber. The droplets ran down Blake's heated cheeks, mingling with her own sweat. Her heart thumped in time with the resonating hum coming from the Tier. Not as manic as it had been back at her apartment, but uncomfortable just the same. Leaving her a little breathless. Her body seemed determined to rattle itself apart.

'Blake, step back. Please.' Weylen stood several metres behind her, waving at her frantically. But Blake shook her head. She couldn't move, even if she wanted to. The water pulled at her, caused the hairs on her arms to stand to attention. As though it wished to drag the liquid in her body back into its fold.

The great funnel of water rose up, like a brilliant emerald twister, and within seconds Tamas became just a faint shadow at the heart of it. Then the carapaces vanished. Everything was hidden behind a churning veil of liquid. The water didn't exceed the circumference of the Tier, but it soared towards the curved roof of the chamber. Far higher than it had done with Azrael's arrival. Blake pressed her earpiece harder against her ear.

'Blake, ready the engagement protocols.' Cym stood at the controls panel behind the glass window of Tech Room Two. 'Prepare the inhibitors.'

She hesitated longer than was necessary, the memory of Cym pushing that serum into her veins still fresh. He couldn't have given her more looks of anguish since, if he'd tried. But still. Pain was pain.

'Technician copies.'

At this stage of proceedings, the carapaces would act as four singular, powerful magnets that would lock on to each of the incoming energy sources. Cym had to time the engagement precisely. Miss the opportunity for lockdown and not only did they risk compromising the energy sources – the gallu – but they risked the entire Facility. The radiation levels at Azrael's Meld, before he had been locked into the carapace, had been dangerously impressive.

'Approaching engagement. Ready for my go-ahead.'

Cym's voice was a disembodied point of calm in the

maelstrom. The Syranians she could see, Bel and Parator, stood with complete ease. Their faces were smooth of any distress or concern. Devoid of anything at all. The same couldn't be said for the small number of humans in the chamber. Three white-suited technicians gathered at her right, faces lit by jade light, their awestruck terror clear in their expressions. Understandable. It was difficult to think of anything but the vibration of the earth, the immense energy that was building in the room. It was impossible to miss. Prickling, electric energy filled the chamber. Pressure before a great thunderstorm. The rumbling of the Tier Waters like a never-ending roll of thunder. Somewhere, in the midst of it all, was Tamas.

Blake blinked, trying to estimate which of the shadows dancing within the chaos was his slight frame. Whatever he might have believed he'd become, a good liar was not it. He'd lied. She'd known him way too long and he was far too transparent for her to have believed him when he'd said that Kira and Azrael had been located. She could forgive Cym for the truth serum; he had as little control of this game as she did. The Syranian did what he could, when he could. Not so different to her. But not Tamas.

She couldn't wipe the image of him listening to her spill her guts. Witnessing her agony and doing nothing to stop it. She thought she'd seen a glimpse of something then. A coldness, a deadness in his eyes that hadn't been evident before. But she'd avoided looking too closely at anyone for so long, she hadn't been sure. When he spat vitriol into her ear before the Meld, it had removed all doubt.

He was lying about having Kira, but he was not lying about wanting to break her.

'I really hope that hurts, you asshole,' Blake whispered.

The shock wave exploded through the chamber, knocking her clear off her feet. The tablet flew from her hand, and the impact with the ground pushed the breath from her lungs. A ripping sound, like a hundred cracks of thunder laid atop one another, tore through the space. Blake cowered beneath raised hands, a paltry defence if the cavern was about to come down on her. It certainly seemed intent on doing so. The funnel of water burst, exploding outward in a shock of jade green. Liquid fireworks sprayed across the chamber. The captain shouted something in the earpiece, but she couldn't make it out. The roaring around her threatened to rupture her eardrums. A huge shape towered over her. It took a moment to register that it was one of the mini cranes – toppling down. Blake cried out, scrambling to get to her feet. A figure body-slammed her, and they tumbled in a mess of limbs. Whoever grasped her, crushed her body against theirs, taking the impact as they hit the hard concrete. They grunted against Blake's ear.

The crane slammed into the ground right alongside them, and concrete chunks flew in all directions.

Green rain poured down on them, plastering Eron's silver hair against his skull.

'Miss Beckworth, are you injured?'

Winded, Blake waved her reply. Eron may have bruised her, but the crane would have killed her. Its impact had created a shallow crater in the concrete.Small pieces of shrapnel rained down on them, pieces of the chamber's rocky ceiling, knocked clear by the force of the shock wave. One struck her on the cheek.

'What happened?' she gasped. 'Are they here?'

'Yet to be determined.'

She pushed herself to her knees. Her earpiece was gone, both it and the communicator dislodged in the tumble. The surface of the Tier was a smooth black. The waters showing no sign of movement, still as a mirror. Of the remaining three cranes, one had toppled in over part of the Tier, its furthermost tip jammed hard against the stonework edging, preventing it from sliding completely into the pool. The second lay overturned, most of it hidden from Blake's view. Parator stood over it, hands outstretched into the air. The third crane had jammed into the narrow space between Tech Rooms One and Two, destroying the observation window of Two, and tearing a slash down the wall of Room One. Dangling between the rectangular rooms was one of the gallu, one of the females, still mostly harnessed into the crane. She thrashed about, tangling herself even more in the wires that bound her. Seder stood over her, no doubt trying to gain some control with the implanted stone in his arm, but his usually benign expression was one of fierce concentration. Beyond him, shadows moved about in Tech Room One, Cym and others still behind the control panels.

The ground beneath Blake rumbled with fresh vibrations, and a low, deep explosion quickly followed. She braced, crouching like a runner at the starting line. But the origins of the explosion were evident. A piece of equipment in Tech Room Two had caught fire, sending an orange glow over Seder and the struggling carapace. Fingers of smoke snaked down around the scene.

Blake got to her feet, and her knees buckled. Eron caught her arm.

'Blake?'

'I'm fine.' She pushed away from his gentle grasp, fighting her own body's reluctance to allow her to stay on her feet. Soaked to the skin, her clothes clinging tightly, her hair like a sodden wig. The temperature had plummeted. 'What the hell just happened?'

'I don't know.'

The crane that had almost crushed her, jerked, the carapace trapped beneath it bucking and writhing.

'Eron.' Bel raced out of the shroud of smoke. 'I'll deal with this one, go to Gren. We've lost contact. Technician, get those inhibitors up and running. Now.'

Eron gave her a short nod and disappeared into the haze.

Blake thought she heard the captain's voice over the calamitous noise still bubbling through the chamber. The smoke from the tech room continued to spread, and the figures around her blurred into shadowy, flitting shapes. Blake coughed, her throat irritated by the hazy air. A high screech rang out through the chamber. Shouts came from somewhere beyond the tech rooms. Blake scoured the ground around her, dizzy at the movement. She could run. Use the chaos to leave the chamber. The Facility. Tempting. But what if she'd been wrong? What if Tamas hadn't been lying, and Kira was here? Somewhere underground, in a Facility that had just been compromised. Rossiter was definitely here. Strapped with Tasers because of her. Blake pressed a hand to her chest. The odd fluttering of her heart was irritating more than anything. As if someone had let birds loose in her chest. She heaved in a breath and held it. Her knees buckled and Blake dropped, throwing her hands out to stop herself from face-planting the concrete.

'Shit.' Blake grimaced. Blood ran from a deep cut at the heart of her left palm. She tugged at the twisted screw embedded there and flung it away.

And that was when she saw him. Tamas. As broken as everything else around her.

She should have raced to him, gone to his side as quickly as Eron had come to hers. Blake remained crouched on the ground, surrounded by the smells and sounds of chaos. A chaos as much her making as his.

It would be right to see if Tamas was still alive. No grey area.

And she should do something definitively right.

Blake staggered to Tamas's body. There was blood – a lot of it – running from a deep gash just below his collarbone. The scalp at his right temple had been ripped back, a hole the size of a stamp leaving bone exposed. Blood glistened on his eyelashes and stained his cheeks. The whites of his eyes showed through the tiny slit of half-open eyelids. Though the bone had not actually pierced through the skin, his left wrist was unequivocally broken. Blake pressed the back of her hand to her mouth, gagging at the memories that rose. Christ, was this how it was going to be? Was Karma was that much of a bitch it would see her argue with everyone she gave a shit about before they died? Left to stare down at the sorry mess she'd made.

Blake jerked her head to one side, just in time for her stomach contents to lurch free. As she retched, guttural cries erupted around her. Shouts and shrieks in English, and sharper calls in the Syranian tongue.

'Blake, Jesus. Are you all right?' Rossiter emerged out of the haze, a piece of cloth pressed to his mouth, muffling his words.

She wiped her mouth. 'What are you doing here?'

'You're bleeding.' Rossiter tried to touch her hand, but she pulled it out of reach.

'I'll live. Is Kira here?'

Kneeling beside Tamas, Rossiter cursed under his breath, touching his fingers to Tamas's bloody neck. 'I don't know. They had me locked up on level two. But the boys aren't assholes. Let me go the minute all the alarms went berserk. He's got a pulse.'

Blake's cloudy mind took a second for his words to register. 'Tamas? He's not dead?'

'Not yet.'

The captain burst through the smoke haze like a willowy giant, towering over them. 'On your feet, Technician.'

He didn't give her an option to comply, or disobey.

Nex hauled her to her feet with none of the gentleness of Eron's grasp. Blake struggled against him. Rossiter rose alongside her. His height didn't compare to the Syranian's, but his bulk still made it a formidable move.

'Take it easy,' he said.

'There's no time to take it easy,' Nex spat. 'We are losing control of the Four. Cym is injured and requires your assistance. The system, what's left of it, is unresponsive. Now move.'

Nex shoved her forward, and a joint in her neck clicked with the force.

'Tamas is dying, how is your god going to like that?' Blake fought against him. 'Losing the precious Messenger can't be a good thing, right?'

Captain Nex released her arm, twisting to look back. When his eyes settled on Tamas, a muscle in his jaw twitched.

'I need two minutes to get him stabilised.' She took a cautious step away. 'Rossiter will get him to medical, but I need to strap his wrist. We're not god-soldiers, not even Tamas. He needs help. Two minutes —'

'Get on with it,' the captain growled. He didn't leave, but he did give them space.

Rossiter frowned as she knelt beside him. 'I could do this,' he muttered.

Reaching for Tamas's broken wrist, Blake breathed against the fresh rise of nausea. 'My townhouse. Bedroom safe, code 1-7-1-1-2-6.' Rossiter gave her a sideways look, recognising the code as the date her world had imploded. 'Take what's in there and protect it, it might be all we have that's worth keeping. That and Azrael. Without them, we're at a gunfight without a gun. You have to find Kira. No way she won't leave a trail somewhere. Try Beleiro.' She was pinning everything on one notion; that she knew her sister well enough to predict Kira's actions. 'Protect them. And do not come back here.'

The Syrana truth serum had not clawed everything from her. Blake had never intended for Kira to go to Melgrove. And there had been no better way to ensure she wouldn't go there, than to order her to a place filled with memories of a dead man.

With Tamas's blood sticky on her skin, Blake rose to her feet and strode after the captain. She had done all she could. Now everything was, quite literally, in Rossiter's hands.

ERON - 19

Radio comms weren't out entirely but were severely distorted. Static was muffling conversations into incoherency. Following Bel's directive, Eron ran around the perimeter of the Tier, headed for the overturned crane that lay on its far side. The bitter scents in the room riled delicate membranes within his sinuses, and the bristling energy still pulsing from the Waters toyed with the layers of his skin. Eron coughed against the discomfort, focusing his attention on not tumbling over the debris scattered in his path.

Within moments he located Gren. The Syranian lay on his back, legs trapped beneath the heavy core of the crane. Eron saw quickly why his brother had not just pulled himself free of the wreckage. A piston from one of the crablike legs that held the crane in place had snapped from its position and speared into his gut. The tubular piece of steel was thick as an arm, piercing the flesh just above Gren's right hip bone. The force it would have taken to propel it through two layers of ballistics armour was equally impressive and horrifying.

'Gren, are you –'

'Eron, just assist me.' Gren gripped the metal impaling him. 'It has gone through to the ground. I can't dislodge it from this angle.'

The Syranians were quick healers, resilient to injuries that would fell other corporeal beings, but they were not immune to pain. Gren would have been in agony. Eron stepped over him, grasped the metal in his hands, and was preparing to attempt to dislodge it when all at once the crane shifted.

'Quickly,' Gren snapped. 'He is rousing.'

For the first time, Eron saw that the gallu was still in the harness at the very end of the crane's arm. He lay a few metres beyond the toppled structure, his upper body free of the harness but one ankle still cuffed into the wide steel clamp at its base. He recognised the creature as the last of the Four shells that Blake had completed. He was as heavyset as Blake's bodyguard Rossiter, and of a similar deepened skin tone, but with a fierceness of face that the human lacked. A faint buzz of blonde hair on his round scalp, a neck that barely existed between broad shoulders, and a square, blunt jaw. Nothing of Azrael's structural fineness remained here. The crane jerked forward, and the movement drew a stifled cry from Gren.

'Did you Bind?' Eron sought purchase on the underbelly of the crane, finding a handhold alongside the tractor tyre, trying to keep the machine still. 'Does the mea hold the gallu?'

'I've done what I can.' Gren hauled at the piston, veins straining in his neck with the effort. 'He is strong.'

'The inhibitors are still not activated?' Eron held fast, but the gallu's movements jolted and shuddered through the metal. Each of the Syranians wore a slender white band at their wrist, designed to allow some sedative control over the gallu in the unlikely event that the telekinetic connection created by the mea stones was not enough.

Gren's brown skin was blotched with rivulets of darker dirt, the Waters still glinting on his eyelashes. 'They aren't responding. He is not responding. He fights it. Fights the mea.'

The inhibitors had proved their strength time and again when used upon Azrael, felling him as though he'd been hit by a sledgehammer. Cym and Blake had found a way to effectively paralyse the gallu within the carapace, or at the very least slow them down considerably, like a human after a few puffs of marijuana. Eron stared at the creature writhing against his restraints. Clearly, this gallu was not remotely stoned.

First priority, though, must be to free Gren from the

tangle.

'I need to disconnect the harness from the crane,' Eron said. 'That will ease your discomfort, give you more strength in the Bind.'

'He is strong, Eron.' Gren's voice was strained. 'I fear he will slip from me. You must be ready.'

Eron nodded, shamed at the rush of exhilaration that came with Gren's words. His brother was wounded, yet Eron thrilled with the idea of attempting a Bind. With a nod towards his fallen brother, Eron braced, waiting for a small moment when the gallu did not struggle so fiercely. There was little doubt Gren would suffer in the time it took for Eron to hurdle the machinery and cut the harness free, so he would bide his time, choose the quietest of moments.

Stillness.

Eron leapt over the low heap of the fallen crane. The gallu's stillness lasted no more than a second. He pushed himself to his new, unfamiliar knees and heaved forward. The crane made a terrible sound against the hard concrete. Eron allowed himself to believe the screech was entirely structural. That it was not mixed with Gren's scream as it wrenched the piston through his gut and dug the crane into his legs. Pulling a knife from a holster at his thigh, Eron swiped down on the tangle of cable at the very tip of the crane arm, seeking to disconnect the harness from the crane itself.

'Gren, are you still with me? Can you hold the Bind?'

Eron took another swipe at the cables. They snapped free and whipped back, barely missing Eron's shoulder.

'Gren,' Eron called again.

No answer. He had to be certain. To attempt a new Bind now could disrupt whatever hold Gren may have – releasing the gallu altogether. The creature itself certainly looked to be free, though. He was on his feet, wavering there much like the intoxicated humans in the night-time establishments Kira had introduced him to. Much like Eron himself had done on more than one occasion. Breathing into that deep well in his mind, Eron reached out tentatively, searching for sign that Gren's Bind with the creature still held. A void greeted him.

The gallu began to move, arms and legs showing little unification. The creature would have been a ridiculous sight if he weren't also so dangerous. The gallu stumbled away.

Eron let out two short exhalations, seeking the cognitive pathway he required. It drifted like a faint memory, protected within its own cortex. An entity in his mind that moved of its own accord. He coaxed it forward, reached for it, and peeled back the folds. The mea connection opened. On his arm, at the stone's locale, there was warmth and little else untoward. But in Eron's skull, it was much like what the humans called a brain freeze. The neurological response of opening to the stone pained nerve endings throughout his face and skull. A headache. Quite unpleasant, if he was truthful.

Eron broke into a run. The creature was moving towards a secondary elevator, a small unit that was used exclusively by Tamas to come and go from his chambers. The gallu lurched about but maintained a good pace.

Eron focused on the mea, readying to unite the stones. Sending a silent prayer to Lahar that he would recall the training correctly, he reached out. Searched. Found. The Bind leapt across the metaphysical void, rapid as any neurological transmission.

The connection of synapses nearly dropped Eron to his knees. He faltered, gathering himself. Gren had not been wrong. The gallu's strength was formidable, far more so than the hapless Azrael. And he was not pleased with the renewed Bind. The gallu reached the elevator doors but did not slow, throwing his considerable weight against them. The Telteriun was a dense metal, the carapaces exceeded half a tonne, and the doors were unlikely to withstand the onslaught. In the end, no onslaught was required. In an unfortunate incident of timing, the elevator doors opened. Inside, two bewildered humans, medics judging by the equipment they held before them like shields, cowered against the back wall of the elevator. Eron hauled at the Bind. The resulting pressure within his skull was enormous. His eyes bulged, and the roar against his eardrums was deafening.

There was some result. The gallu did falter, his thick legs buckling for a moment. One of the humans managed to sidestep the staggering gallu and ran out of the elevator. His companion was not so fortunate. A stinging sensation whiplashed through Eron's mind, and his tenuous hold on the Bind collapsed. Warm liquid filled his nostrils. The gallu stepped into the elevator and grabbed the human, lifting the woman easily and hurling her out into the chamber. Her scream soared into the smoky air, ending a few moments later when she hit the concrete with a crack and thump that spoke of broken bones. Eron took a step towards her, then corrected himself. Admonished himself. She was not his concern.

Standing in the centre of the elevator, the gallu arched its back and made the first sound with its constructed vocal chords. A guttural sound that might have been from a wild animal. Something burst from his back, filling the confines of the space.

Appendages that looked to be wings.

'By Lahar's great blessing, what are . . .' Eron breathed out the words, letting them die on the air unfinished.

The creature twisted, trying to turn and see what protruded from his own back. The wings, tubular lengths of metal alloy, were too big for the confined space. Knife-like points formed each tip and made light work of the innards of the elevator, shredding metal around the creature as he twisted and turned. The gallu launched upwards with breathtaking speed, and half a tonne of Telteriun cannonballed up through the thin ceiling. The wings were the last things to disappear into the elevator shaft.

Eron was about to lose the gallu.

He swore, letting go a stream of Kira's favourite expletives. The thought of her bolstered him. Not with pleasant recall, but the realisation that this was the very moment he could prove his loyalty, his dedication. Show his worth. To his captain, and his Lord.

Eron let his desperation fill him, let it bloom into something greater and harder. Let it drive the Bind out into the void and lash around the creature that sought to disgrace him. The desperation melted into something dark, buoyed by the many solitary days he'd endured, the banishment and the shame. The disappointment.

Though the gallu was lost from view, Eron sensed the upward motion of the creature as he made his way up the shaft. Eron sought greater purchase, body straining with the effort of increasing his hold on the Bind. His lips were warm and damp, fluid streaming from his nose. But he held fast. The gallu fought, but Eron fought harder.

Slowly, but most definitely surely, the Bind began to drag the creature back down the shaft. And desperation turned to exhilaration. The shade inside Eron grew, an ire that tightened the muscles of his chest. The gallu's resistance grew weaker with every tightening of the Bind. And with one final sharp tug, Eron wrenched the creature back through the gaping hole he had made in the elevator roof. The heavy humanoid shell hit the floor, his shape indented into the surface. No sign of the curving arches of metal he had borne from his back. Eron stood over the gallu, chest heaving. A lust filled him, a puissant desire to crush any will that remained inside the construct. The Bind bristled with power. *His* power. Eron curled up his fists, muscles twitching with the urge to lash out. The gallu stared up at him. He lay completely still, with not so much as a twitch of a finger or the rise of chest with breath, but his gaze held Eron. Drew him in. A gleam of intimacy and darkness there in the creature's eyes. Eron could not look away, did not want to.

'Eron.'

The captain's voice was chilled water to the face. Eron stepped away from the gallu with an odd sense of guilt.

'Sir, I've –'

The captain gestured for him to be silent. Eron opened his mouth, angry words ready for expulsion. He immediately checked himself. He'd never spoken a harsh word to the captain's face, yet here he found himself with a tirade on his tongue. He took another step away from the gallu, refusing to meet the gaze he felt still upon him. The captain was oblivious, listening in on his communicator. Eron searched for his own, pulling it from where it had tangled around the back of his neck. Pushing it to his ear, he heard Blake Beckworth's voice clear through the device.

' . . . all are operational. His levels indicate containment paralysation. Can you confirm?'

The captain glanced at him. Eron nodded, his mood sinking with realisation. He had overblown his own strength in the subjugation. The gallu had not lain so still at his feet for fear of Eron. He had been locked in by the inhibitors.

'Confirmed.' Eron entered the conversation. 'The gallu is subdued.'

'That's the final.' Blake's robotic voice crackled through the heavy static. 'All four carapaces now contained.'

She disconnected and the dreadful interference vanished. Eron and the captain stood facing one another. Shouts rang out around them as a team surrounded the burning tech room, subduing the flames with retardants. Blood seeped into Eron's mouth, his nose still flowing. And strands of his hair stuck to his cheeks. But Eron stood to attention, awaiting his orders.

Captain Nex eyed the fallen gallu, his expression, as always, impossible to decipher.

'You will Bind with this one until Gren is restored.'

The oxygen rushed from Eron's lungs, making it difficult to force the words free. 'Captain, yes, sir. Thank you.'

The captain moved further into the smoke haze, lifting a hand as he disappeared. 'Look at what surrounds you. It is not a gift, Eron. Do your duty.'

Duty, gift, it didn't matter. Not in this moment. This blessed moment. Eron wiped at his face, pushing back the sodden silver strands plastered to his cheeks. His smile was impossible to wipe clear, despite the chaotic mess surrounding him.

Gren's recovery was inevitable. The fortitude granted to the god-soldiers by the Lord Lahar ensured that, but in the interim Eron would work to ensure no doubt remained of his worthiness. Eron crouched down beside the gallu, intending to inform the creature of how they would be the victorious Bind. The pair who brought Dumuzi to their gods.

The utterance died in his throat.

The gallu watched him, eyes filled again with that same gleam of intimacy. A hint of a secret shared. A calling into the sullen, dark depths.

Eron rose to his feet and walked away, quickening his stride as he went.

KIRA - 20

The dreams were as boring as they were horrific. Same shit, at least once a week. She was behind the wheel, her hands melted to the leather, skin stuck fast. Unable to pull free when the world-eating tree loomed up ahead.

Kira bolted upright. Catapulting back into the real world. 'Balls, shit, fuck.'

The air stank with something burning, making her gag. 'No, no.' She lunged for the door handle, every muscle in her back jabbing a sharp protest against her spine.

'Kira.' The voice, soft and low and right there, pulled her up. 'There is no harm.'

A hand on her shoulder. And for the splittiest of split seconds, she imagined it was Eron. He'd been here enough times. Dragging her out of a nightmare. His baby-butt-soft skin pressed against hers till she stopped sweating like a Swede in a sauna. Kira's fingers traced the tear in the fabric where the handle had been. Remembering how it had come free when she'd decided she'd had enough of the rattling blue Datsun. Her skin wasn't melted to anything. She was free. Kira swivelled round.

'Hey, Az. All good.' Not as pretty as Eron, but eye candy just the same. Kira tucked a couple of wayward curls behind her ear. Shit, she must look like a million dollars. And what the fuck was that smell? They were still in the car, pulled up in a driveway in front of a faded yellow house, and they were the only passengers. 'Where are the Loony Two?'

Azrael gave her a look, the confused one he still favoured despite now being able to hold coherent conversations.

'The woman and the kid,' she said. 'Leona, Vail, you know, the ones we've been in a car with for hours?'

Azrael pointed out the front window. The wooden house was desperate for a paint job, a single-story example of home maintenance gone bad. The roof of the narrow front veranda had more skylights than actual roof. There were lights on inside. One of the front windows was mostly masking-tape strips, with a piece of glass here and there. Silhouetted by the internal lights, a woman with a shock of white hair stared out at them.

'Oh god, she's still here. What time is it? Jesus.' Kira rubbed at her neck. 'Why are we still in the car? You're housetrained, didn't you tell her?' Kira smiled at her own joke. Azrael did not. No surprises there. He held what looked like a small and very sad bouquet of dead things. Sticks and clearly long-since-picked flowers and grasses. Quite possibly the source of the smell which was making her stomach churn.

'You were sleeping,' he said. 'You did not wake when we arrived. I did not want them to wake you. I have stayed with you.'

Fair enough. Straight to the point. Kira rubbed the sides of her mouth, fingers finding wetness. Great. She'd been drooling. Probably farted too; champagne made her do that. Poor bastard.

'What's with the death bouquet?' It was dark out, not full-on night-time, but getting damn close.

'Leona asked me to hold this, as I wished to remain with you.'

First-name-basis buddies now. Sweet.

'She did, huh? Any particular reason? 'Cause I can tell you now that if you're going to ask me on a date, it's really not the time.'

Azrael's confused look returned. The guy managed to look hot as all hell even when he frowned. 'It is to hide my brightness. I believe she may be able to understand who I am.'

'Oh fuck, the witchy stuff again.' Kira sighed. Any hope this was all a part of her bad dreams flew out the window. 'Tell me there are no frogs' legs in that pile of crap.'

Maybe decaying frogs' legs smelled like badly burnt cinnamon buns.

'No frogs' legs.'

The voice at the open window made her jerk in her seat. 'Holy shit, Vail. Don't sneak up on people unless you want to make them crap themselves.'

It still pissed her off, how her heart didn't so much as flutter when she got shit-scared or, on the incredibly rare occasion, ran somewhere. Even when waking from the car-crash nightmares, the chunk of metal in her chest just did its silent thing. No beat. No thump. Pumping the blood through her a little faster if need be. But always quiet as death.

'Sorry. We saw you were awake. Leona sent me out.' Vail ducked his head, and his heavy blunt fringe fell into his eyes. 'It's probably best you come in now.'

Kira's guts rumbled, punctuating the point. And it was pee-break time again. Jesus, was her bladder the size of a pea? Fucking felt like it. The last stop, at a fast-food joint, had been at least a couple of hours ago. The kid had packed away three double bacon cheeseburgers, fries, and a thick shake. He was a hollow reed, apparently. Kira climbed out of the car, her butt aching and her neck muscles so pissed off it wasn't funny.

'How are you feeling?' Vail asked, puppy-dog eyeing her. Giving a shit about her day, despite the catastrophic way his had turned out. He was either completely fucked up or a goddamn angel.

'Great. It's been a great day.' Probably wanted for murder about now, too. There was that to deal with. Great day. Christ. 'You? How you doing?'

Did she give a toss? Kinda yeah, which was incredibly annoying. Too much crap going on to care about a kid who looked as though he were out of some cutesy anime. Complete with impossibly sad eyes and a forlorn air of lostness.

'I've had better.' His voice cracked on the 'better', but he offered her a smile. Fake as all hell, but ten points for effort.

'Yeah, I hear you, kid.'

She needed to get Az back to the Facility. Let Blake deal with this fallout. Dumbest fucking idea ever to let Kira play with her toys.

'Lead the way.' She put on a too-bright smile. Surely this house had a land-line. Carrier pigeon, smoke signals. Something. 'Take us to your leader.'

Inside, the house was almost as cluttered as the car. She edged sideways down the hall to get past piles of random junk;

everything from a baby bath to an old vacuum cleaner made the pathway an obstacle course. And the house didn't smell much better than the car. Wait. No. Correct that. The house smelled far more disgusting. They walked into the kitchen, and the waft of cabbage hit her square in the face.

'Christ almighty.' She pressed her sleeve over her mouth and nose. 'What's that supposed to do? Ward off anyone with sinuses?'

'It protects us, you ungrateful girl.' Leona wiped her hands on a lace-trimmed apron that was yellow as Big Bird. 'Vera Melsy is pretty OCD with warding her house, but I think we are going to need even more than she has on offer.'

'Who the hell is Vera?'

'The woman whose house this is.' Spoken like Kira was a dickhead for not knowing already.

'We broke into a house?'

'Of course not. Stupid girl.'

'Fuck you.'

'No thank you,' Leona replied nonchalantly, as though Kira had just offered her a cup of tea. 'Vera is a friend, from a long time ago. We were part of the same Rudiment once. She's also in Mongolia and has left her spare key in the same place for about the last ten years.'

'Good old Vera.' Kira slumped into a chair at the dining

table in the centre of the room. Both the table and the chair were rickety. 'Does Vera have a phone?'

'Who would you call if she did? Your sister?' Leona opened the pantry, rummaging through its contents and stepping back with a cask of red wine in hand. Kira sent up a silent prayer to the god of grape and grain that it was for her. 'For years I've been telling all the Rudiments the Facility wasn't right. I've been telling people for years. Now, perhaps they will pay attention. I don't know how you got out of that place, but it might well be the most useful thing you've ever done, Kira Beckworth.'

Okay. Forget the red. Kira stood up. They knew who she was, where she and Azrael were from. They had followed her to the Wheel and Barrow, then somehow followed her to the casino. She had gotten in a car with them and driven to god knows where. It suddenly all felt like a really, really fucking stupid idea.

'Thank you for the compliment,' Kira said. 'That means so much coming from a crazy fucking witch.'

Leona actually tut-tutted. 'We descend from the Wiccan, but I am not a witch. We are the Disciples of the Maiden, the force of nature that lies all around you. If you took your head out of a bottle, you might notice it. The power behind a storm, the energy inherent in a flash of lightning, the

fury of a volcano, or the earth-breaking swell of an earthquake
–'

'Jesus. Preach to someone who gives a shit. Just give me a goddamn phone.'

Leona's eyes couldn't have gotten any wider if she'd held her eyelids open herself. 'You, young lady –'

'Leona, it's okay.' Vail entered the room carrying a tablet with some straw-hatted anime character sticker plastered on the back of it. The lizard perched on the kid's shoulder, bulgy black eyes watching Azrael. 'You can see she doesn't know about any of this. Give her time.'

Time? For what? *Keep him away from here, no matter what you might hear.* Words straight from Blake's mouth. But did that include hearing someone scream as they fell twenty-five stories out a glass window? What exactly was Kira keeping Azrael away from? She had no money to call a cab. And stealing the car wasn't an option.

'Well, she should know,' Leona sniffed. 'Why is she walking around with a bright one if she has no clue –'

'Because my stupid bloody sister asked me to!' Kira dropped back into her chair, and thumped her forehead against the tabletop. This was the worst trip she'd been on, and she was stone-cold sober. A hand rested on her shoulder. 'I'm okay, Az. Just losing it.'

She sat up. Sure enough, Azrael's hand rested on her shoulder. As she knew it would. Vail stood just as close, clutching his laptop, but Kira would have bet her overworked liver on it being Azrael touching her.

'What is happening?' she groaned, forehead hitting the tabletop again.

There was movement around her, a bit of whispering.

'Do something, Leona.'

'Fine, don't get your knickers in a knot, boy. Here, have some of this. Calm your nerves.' Something slammed down onto the table beside Kira's head. And the sweet, sweet scent of red wine found its way through the stench. Kira lifted her head, chin resting on the table edge. A pint glass of crimson goodness sat a few centimetres away. Her hand moved before her thoughts did. Glass in hand she took a long, slow swig. Shiraz. Nothing fancy but it shat all over the house red they stocked at the Wheel and Barrow. Oh, Perry. What she wouldn't do to be getting shit-faced at work right now.

'What do you know of me?' Az spoke in a low, almost sultry whisper. He moved up close to Leona, and she raised her hands. At first Kira thought it was a defensive move. Nope. Kinda the opposite. Her hands fluttered over his chest, her breathing quickening. Kira took another sip.

'Nothing personal but it's best I keep a distance.' If the

room hadn't been dead silent, Kira might not have heard Leona at all, she spoke so softly. 'We're going to need help to decipher you. You nearly blew my eyes out of their sockets last time we touched.'

'Oh Christ.' Kira took another longer, harder gulp. 'Your lines need work, love. When you're finished fan-girling, can we go to a room that doesn't smell of rotten ass?'

Vail stifled a smile. Apparently seeing her about to puke was something he found funny.

But Leona and Az were locked in a stare-fest. 'Do you recall nothing of your origin?'

'I do not,' Azrael said. 'Do you know who I am?'

His hands were raised as though he was fighting to stop himself from touching her. Nothing nefarious. Just desperate. And the ache of it slammed a fist into Kira's cold, hard, metal heart. Her own ache this time. Good old pain-in-the-ass empathy.

The woman's expression softened, and Kira bit her lip, bracing for the reply she saw coming.

'No. I don't. I'm sorry.' Leona winced. 'But I do believe I know where you are from.'

Vail placed the laptop on the table and darted a glance at Leona before clearing his throat. 'Azrael, you might want to take a look at this. See if it means anything to you.'

The lizard made a chirruping sound. Kira blinked, sure she'd just seen the thing nod its teeny, grotesque dragon head.

'Az can't eat soup or drink beer,' Kira said. 'He's hardly going to be able to read.'

'Still, it might be worth taking a look.' Vail tapped at the keys, swiping his finger across the touchscreen, eyes so narrowed they looked closed. 'Help him remember who he is.'

'There's internet here?' Kira said. Internet meant Skype. Or, at the very least, email. *Ready or not, Blake, here we come.* But her question was ignored. Leona pulled out a chair and gestured for Az to sit. He did, and Leona and Vail gathered around him, forcing Kira onto tiptoes to get a look at the screen. The web page's flowery text declared that this site knew everything there was to know about Sumerian mythology. The entire page was mostly writing in a tiny font that would have been a bitch to try to read. There were a couple of pictures, though. One caught Kira's eye. Some naked chick with clawed feet and great boobs held a staff in one hand, a small cup in the other, and had wings the length of her body draped at her sides.

Big Boobs was called Ereshkigal, apparently.

'Ereshkigal, what kind of friggin' name is that? Okay, what are we looking at? Az was an ancient Playboy Bunny?'

Leona puffed out a breath. 'Ereshkigal is the queen of the underworld. The Sumerians worshipped her —'

'Sumerians? Like in Jesus's time or something?' Kira said, draining more wine.

'No, much earlier,' Vail said. 'We're talking beginning of civilisation and –'

'So what the hell has she got to do with Az?'

Azrael stared at the screen, but nothing showed on his face to betray what he was thinking. Quite possibly nothing at all. The guy had learned to talk all of five minute ago.

'Oh by the Maiden's laces, will you shut up and listen, girl?' Leona shoved the cask across the table. 'Occupy yourself with this, but listen. When we exorcised those possession spirits at the hotel –' She gave Vail a sideways glance and continued. 'I obtained some information. A sense, if you like, of their identities, and their intentions.'

'Aside from strangling me, and humping Az, that was what?' Kira ran her finger round the rim of her glass.

Vail shifted in his seat, turning to look up at her. 'There was a lot of confusion. They seemed as surprised as we were to find them there. Like they didn't quite know what to do once they found some bodies to inhabit, didn't know what to do with their own strength.'

'They claimed they were utukku.' Leona stirred the bubbling pot with slow circulations. 'Not a title I was familiar with, but I had my suspicions. We wanted an opportunity to research before we told you anything. That Azrael is a bright one is evident –'

'You keep saying that, and I keep having no clue.' Kira refilled her pint glass.

'A supermundane, a preternatural –'

'Oh yeah, he's super all right.'

Leona paused with her stirring. 'You understand. I know you do. I saw your face when he touched you. He is a supernatural being, and those utukku believed he would be able to return them to their true realm. Azrael is ripe with a raw power, the like of which I've never witnessed. And that power does not come from the Maiden. She herself is a fledgling, her full strengths are still developing. A new god whose Dawning is yet to come. We worship at her altar, awaiting that day when she emerges from the Earth and graces us –'

Vail coughed, interrupting the sermon. 'These utukku, if that's what they are, are ancient. Thousands of years old, and there's been no hint of them before now. There are a few supermundanes that pop up every now and then, but very basic stuff, wood sprites, weaker stuff like that. Nothing like this.'

'Of course.' Kira chugged wine.

'These utukku were off the charts . . . Azrael is off the charts. And for whatever reason, they thought he was their ticket home. They are trapped here, we think, but have been dormant until now.'

Rubbing her eyes, Kira debated asking the question. Decided what the hell? Sanity had gone to hell in a handbasket anyway. 'Ticket home?'

'To Kur. The underworld.' Vail nodded at the screen. 'Where that goddess rules.'

'Oh, right. That makes sense now.' Kira slapped her thigh. 'Az is some kind of demon lord of the underworld. That was my second guess after advanced AI. Guess those prayer-loving ali –'

She caught herself in time. About to mention the A word. One big reveal at a time, she decided. Things were complicated enough without mentioning the ETs.

Az, the man . . . being . . . android . . . whatever-the-fuck, sat staring at Big Boobs.

'Recognise her, Az?'

Slow shake of the head, side to side, not lifting his eyes from the screen. Bradley the freaky lizard jumped off Vail's shoulder, landing on the keyboard beside Azrael's hand. Az didn't flinch. Still as a statue.

Leona rapped the metal spoon against the side of the pot. 'We don't know who or what he is, but those possession spirits believed him to be a creature of Kur. Explains why our workings were magnified so dangerously.' Vail's enthusiasm slid off his face like a mask, but Leona kept going. 'Azrael's energy radiates, and these utukku will not be the last who are drawn to him. He's a magnet for supermundanes of all sorts. We need to get you to the Rudiment in Jackson.'

'Please god, tell me that's a nightclub, somewhere there are lots of drugs.' Kira refilled her pint glass.

'The Disciples of the Maiden are all formed into Rudiments. Groups, really. You'd probably call them covens.' Vail puppy-eyed her from beneath his bangs. 'It's usually based on geographical locations, but we kind of got booted out of the local one –'

'I got expelled.' Leona poured herself a glass of red into a giant coffee mug that declared, *I believe in unicorns*. 'Vail suffered because they sought to be rid of me.'

Vail gave her an indulgent smile. 'Leona's right about the Rudiment, though. William runs it, and he'll take us in. You'll be safe there. William will be able to help us work out what's going on.'

All the sweet, doe-eyed looks in the world weren't going to see that happen. 'Sounds like a barrel of laughs, and William sounds like a great guy. But I'm not moving another inch until I speak to my sister.'

The lizard barked, and the frill of his collar expanded around his beady-eyed face.

'What's wrong with slimy?' Kira glared at the reptile.

Leona sniffed. 'Bradley is not slimy, he's a *Tylototriton anguliceps*. Very rare. And I believe he thinks contacting your sister is a very bad idea. As do we all. She asked you to take Azrael from the Facility, didn't she? What exactly did she tell you to do with him?'

Kira folded her arms across her belly and walked across the cracked vinyl floor to the window. A sliver of moon rose above a poorly lit street. In the silence, the laptop pinged with an incoming message.

'She said . . .' Kira spotted a rotary phone propped on a pile of magazines, half-hidden by a faded floral curtain. 'She said . . . shit . . .'

She couldn't call Blake. A super spy Kira was not, but a dumb-ass could work out that contacting her sister at a place that designed high-end surveillance and robotic tech for the military was probably a stupid idea. Blake knew when Kira fucked someone on a beach half a world away; tracing a phone call would be child's play.

Blake wanted Az kept hidden. Kira was on her own. With an utukku-attracting, underworld-dwelling, million-dollar piece of tech, that might be a demon. Kira sighed.

'She told me to keep him away from the Facility. No matter what I heard.'

The words lifted from her, heaving a great weight with them. Maybe she was just as nuts as the two witches behind her, but goddamn it felt good to share the load.

'Oh no,' Vail breathed.

'Oh shit,' Leona said.

'Oh yes.' Kira leaned on the windowsill watching the wind play with a brass chime hanging from the veranda. 'You have no idea how much I wish I'd told Blake to fuck off –'

'Kira, that's not what we meant,' Vail said.

The lizard barked again, little snaps of sound, like a chihuahua with a bad cold. Kira turned. Vail's face had dropped a shade or two of pale. Leona glared at the laptop screen, hands on her hips.

'What's wrong?'

'We keep tabs on the Facility, any newsfeeds about the place –' Vail began.

Leona shoved past Kira as she raced back to the table.

'And? What did you see?'

Vail spun the screen. The website was The Smoking Gun. Ironically, one of the same conspiracy-theory-loving sites that Blake had told her once the Facility kept tabs on, tracking how close to the truth anyone was getting about proving the existence of the Syranians. The nutters had been convinced for years the aliens were in the basement, luckily, no one paid much attention to a sad bunch of people who believed the moon landing was a fake.

But people might pay attention to an explosion at the Facility. One large enough to register low-level seismic activity at the nearest monitoring station.

'Shit. Blake.' Kira's wine-laden stomach turned. 'Fuck what she said, we have to go to the Facility.'

Glass clanged and cupboard doors thumped as Leona piled things into a wicker picnic basket that had seen better days. 'I'm sure she's fine. They say she's a genius.' Leona grunted, heaving a giant jar of pickles from an overhead cupboard. 'You can't go to the Facility. We have to go to the Rudiment. Now.'

'Like hell —'

The laptop pinged again. Vail opened a new tab, and a headline blazed across the screen. Apparently Leona and Vail didn't just keep an eye on the Facility.

'You are fucking kidding me.' Kira stared at her own face on the screen next to a headline that read 'Kira Beckworth Linked to Casino Murder?'

The picture, one from a year ago on a beach in Greece, ran alongside a video of the two guys in the elevator, the drunk touchy-feely lovebirds, who were loving every second of their fifteen minutes of fame as a local news crew questioned them about the casino murders. Spouting off about how they'd chatted with Kira Beckworth in the elevator as she was headed to the penthouse floor. How certain they were that it was her, despite the wig and glasses, because they'd spotted her chest tattoo through her ludicrously expensive designer shirt. How concerned they were when they heard about the death, assuming one of her parties had gotten out of hand.

Miffed they hadn't gotten an invite.

'Oh, those two have very big mouths.' Leona hustled in alongside her. There was no actual footage of Kira in the hotel. Whatever hoodoo-voodoo stuff Az had going on had buggered up every camera they'd gone near. The authorities were clutching at straws, but it was a big hotel, with an enormous wallet, and it wanted its reputation straightened out.

'They want to question Kira about the . . . accident.' Vail's fingers shook over the keyboard.

'Oh shit,' Leona said.

Kira frowned at her own smiling face. Tanned and high, and a lifetime away from all this. 'All the shit, all the fans.'

'What do we do?' Vail said.

'Plan A, we get wasted.' Kira tapped her empty glass. 'And pretend none of this is happening.'

Azrael pressed his hands against the table and rose to his feet. 'We go to the Rudiment, where the Disciples of the Maiden can offer protection, and source my true identity.'

Kira reached for the cask of wine. 'I'm going to stick with Plan A. Anyone else with me?'

Without a word, Leona thrust out her half-empty coffee mug, and this time there was no doubt in Kira's mind that the lizard nodded.

Ready for more?

The *Metal Angels* serial continues…

Part Two coming *13 July, 2018.*

Subscribe to **daniellekgirl.com** and be first
to know when pre-orders go live!

**Reviews are awesome! The more the merrier. Don't forget to
leave me a quick review wherever you bought your copy. I'd
love to read what you think.**